ONLY DARK EDGES

KATIE L. CARROLL

To the ones we've lost—
And the ones left behind
Who are there for each other

Act I

"And yet to me, what is this quintessence
of dust?"

William Shakespeare
Hamlet
Act II, Scene II

Chapter 1

Grief is a storm that churns deep inside me. Others can't see it, but they can sense it—even those who don't know I've lost someone.

Today everyone here knows I've lost Gemma. My sister. My best friend. My twin-not-twin.

I stand facing the long line of mourners, my mom and stepdad next to me and on the other side of them, Gemma's casket. A small comfort that my parents decided on a closed casket because the idea of Gemma's lifeless face and body laid bare for all to see makes me want to throw up.

While everyone here knows of our loss, none of them see what it's doing to me.

They can't see the winds that wrap around my heart, swirling tighter and tighter until it strains to beat against the gale. They can't touch the rain that fills my lungs, slowly drowning me in my own feelings.

But if they looked into my eyes long enough, they might get a flash of lightning. The flickering light sparking something ugly inside of me.

If they listened closely, they might hear the rumble of thunder deep in my churning belly. The resonant sound threatening to burst and incapacitate all around me.

If they looked.

The problem is that no one wants to stare directly into the storm of grief. Their gazes brush across the surface, sense the turmoil inside, and recoil. A protective instinct that allows them to think it will prevent them from the same fate of suffering. Or keep them from remembering their own losses.

I don't blame them. I wish I could do the same. Offer up my condolences and move on with my day, my life, pretend like nothing tragic has touched me.

I can't because I'm trapped from the inside by this storm. Slowly, silently spinning away from reason. Wishing someone would stop and notice I'm drowning.

But drowning doesn't always look like drowning. The one time I almost drowned for real there were no flailing arms or cries for help. It was a stillness, a glassy-eyed look. It was barely keeping above water, face tilted toward the sky. Surviving but barely.

That's me now, only the water isn't surrounding me. It's inside me.

The ones who are supposed to notice, who should be there to throw me a life preserver, are stuck in the storm of their own grief.

So it's me and this storm. And I don't know how long I can contain it before it spins out of me and rips a path of destruction through my life, destroying anyone who dares to get close.

Chapter 2

I have survived a whole summer without Gemma.

Being not quite a full year apart, we called each other twin-not-twin. Other people called us Irish twins because for seven days every year—from my birthday on March 15 until hers on March 22—we were the same age.

Though Gemma would always argue that having just turned an age and almost the next age are not the same. But for one glorious week, my smile was always a little bit bigger because my sister and I had something special in common: our age.

My next birthday will be the last time I'm the same age as Gemma. And once the birthday after that comes, I'll forever be older than my big sister.

These are the thoughts that keep me up at night. Tonight, on the eve of my junior year and what would have been Gemma's senior year, I lie awake and miss my sister so badly, it's a physical pain deep in my chest.

It's no surprise the first word I ever spoke was "sister." I worshiped Gemma from the moment I met her.

I was only hours old when she came to the hospital to first see me. She spent most of her time playing on the floor with a giant stuffed bear that was her big-sister present. She went to hug the bear, missed, and bonked her head on the floor. Gemma cried so hard, two nurses came rushing in. My mom put me in the little newborn bed and scooped up Gemma. I was also screaming by then, so one of the nurses tried to comfort me.

Nothing worked to soothe either of us, and eventually,

we ended up on the bed next to each other. The story goes that I instantly stopped crying and put a chubby little hand on Gemma's face. She quieted too and then started singing, not actual words because she was too young for that, but in the way that an almost one-year-old does.

My mom said I stared up at her with wide eyes, and I've barely looked away since.

And now I haven't seen her face for two whole months. Tonight, along with the pain in my chest, the storm inside me is restless but manageable, less a hurricane and more a rumbling summer storm.

It's not my parents who have tempered the storm; they're still figuring out how to tread water themselves. Or my best friend, Jasmine, who has offered me little solace this summer. She looked up to Gemma almost as much as I did, and every time we've hung out, it's been the saddest pity party ever.

It's certainly not Camille. She still goes by the title of Gemma's best friend, but that traitorous bitch doesn't deserve it.

Gemma, Jasmine, Camille, and I used to be an inseparable foursome. We were branches of the same tree, but the gale force winds of Gemma's death have ripped us apart and tossed around the pieces until we're little more than matchsticks littering the ground.

No, it's my girlfriend, Emberly, that has kept the storm at bay. She briefly met my sister, who died right after Emberly moved to town. Somehow, it's easier to be around someone who never really knew Gemma than to be with the people who knew her best.

Emberly is untethered as well, but in a totally different way. I'm caught up in an awful cycle of grief, while she's trying to adjust to changing schools for her senior year.

She's a swimmer, like Gemma was, and will be on the varsity team with Jasmine and Camille. Not me. It was a running joke among the inseparable foursome that I was the only one who wasn't a gifted swimmer. The best I can do is dog paddle across the pool. Figures that I'd fall for a swimmer.

I roll over in my bed and face the wall so I don't have to stare at the empty bed across our room.

My room…alone.

I talk to Gemma at night when I can't sleep, which is most nights.

"Gemma, can you hear me?" I whisper to the wall. It's quiet enough that if someone pressed their ear to the door, they wouldn't hear it, but hopefully loud enough that Gemma's soul—or whatever is left of her—can sense it.

I've asked this question every night since she died. Before, I wasn't sure if I believed in an afterlife, but I do now. My last shred of sanity would evaporate faster than a puddle in the height of summer if I believed otherwise. A universe where Gemma doesn't exist in some form is one I can't fathom.

I sense her presence, too. She was there in the purple phlox that bloomed in the back garden the day she died. She was there on the beach when Camille, Jasmine, and I went body-surfing and I almost drowned. That was before I found out about Camille's betrayal.

Gemma's body has gone to ashes, tucked inside a sturdy little black box because our mother can't bear to pick out a real urn or scatter her ashes, but something of her still exists. That's who I whisper to at night…and hope for an answer. Or a sense of peace. Or maybe some closure.

Tonight I squeeze my eyes shut, deciding which of the

details of my day to share with Gemma.

"School starts tomorrow." I swallow through a throat thick as honey straight from the comb. "It was supposed to be our year. We were going to dominate the school."

We had so many plans for the year where we'd both be upperclassmen. It was going to be the best year ever.

I sigh and roll back to face her empty bed, easy enough to see with the streetlight creeping in behind the curtain on her side of the room because I didn't bother to close the blinds.

Gemma's bed is covered in the yellow and white afghan our grandmother made. It has the same herringbone pattern as my green and white one. I've spent enough time in her bed this summer to know my sister's blanket still smells like her, honeysuckle body lotion with a hint of chlorine. One of the downfalls of being a swimmer is the lingering scent of pool water that seems to cling to the skin no matter how many times you've showered.

"Gemma, why aren't you here?" My melancholy turns to anger. "Can you even fucking hear me?"

She used to always give me big eyes when I would drop f-bombs. Not that she was against swearing, but she said she couldn't get used to them coming out of her little sister's mouth. I would be quick to remind her that I'm barely her *little* sister.

I miss that look, and arguing with her. I miss so much.

The storm of grief stirs my insides, makes my stomach ache and sets my teeth on edge. It's exhausting holding it back, but sleep still does not come.

As I wait for an answer that also never comes, light glints off the jar of sea glass on Gemma's nightstand. We collected each and every one of those pieces ourselves, our most prized one a small red piece in the shape of a lopsided heart. I can't tell what the source of the reflected light is, and it almost looks like the light is coming from the jar itself.

A breeze rustles the curtains near her bed, though I'm sure that window is closed. My stepdad works in heating and cooling and one of the few things my parents have splurged on is central air. The mysterious breeze blows over to my side of the room, bringing with it the fetid stench of low tide. I choke back a gag as my eyes water, the numbers on my bedside clock blurring as they click to midnight.

The gag turns into a gasp as a figure forms on my sister's bed and whispers, "Delta."

Tonight I may just get the answers to all the questions I've been asking.

Chapter 3

"Gemma?" I sit up, clutch the afghan to my chest.

"Yesss." The word hisses on the rancid breeze.

The curtain stops rustling and the jar of sea glass is shrouded in darkness once more. The ghostly figure of my sister sits on her bed. I must be dreaming. I must have dozed off without realizing it and now I'm asleep and dreaming of Gemma.

It's the worst kind of dream. I've been having them a lot. Where Gemma is here and alive, but I can feel something is wrong, a nagging sensation that tells me this isn't possible. Yet I can never get beyond the feeling to identify the problem. It's like my brain can't allow me to have this break from grief without tapping on my heart to remind me that she's not supposed to be here, but it can only do so in the vaguest of ways.

It's the worst when I wake. The crush of remembering that my sister is not here and never will be again. And I wasn't even able to enjoy having her there in the dream. The grief storm never lets me rest, not even in sleep.

But tonight I'm too acutely aware of everything to believe this is a dream. I pinch my forearm and squeak when it hurts, confirming I'm awake.

"Delta," the voice comes again. It's breathy but distinctly Gemma. With it comes the stench of decay.

How many times in our 16 years of sharing this room have I heard her whisper my name? How many times in these last two months have I longed to hear it again? And here it is now, but instead of filling me with hope and warmth, I'm left with a cold pit of dread in my stomach.

"Gemma," I say again, like it's the only word I know.

"I'm here." Her body blinks off and then on again in a slightly different position, posed on her side, head propped up on a hand. A position I've seen her in a million times. The figure is ethereal—I can see the curtains and window through it—but it's there.

"Gemma!" I'm a playlist of one word stuck on repeat... a playlist of madness if I really believe that I'm seeing her ghost. It must be the lack of sleep and my stormy stomach catching up with me. It's driven me to full-on hallucinations. "How are you...? What...?"

My thoughts stutter along with my words. Images of Gemma's body in a casket, looking like her but also not, flit through my mind. Her hands holding a single rose. Her eyes closed as if in sleep, but me knowing they will never open again. Images that aren't real because her funeral was closed casket.

It has me questioning what is real and what isn't.

My feet find the carpet of their own accord and take me toward her. Her tenuous form sits up as I approach. I join her on the bed but not too close, keeping to the very end. While there's not a wrinkle below her, my weight pushes down into the mattress and messes up the blanket. I long to brush her hair and have her brush mine as we used to do on this very spot. Tentatively, I reach out, but she shies away, and I halt in midair. Would there be anything for me to feel if I tried to touch her?

"Pleassse, don't," she says. "Remember my touch as it was when I was warm."

The stench emanating from this ghost is foul. I'm reminded of digging for clams, the squishy wet sand in between my fingers and the funk of low tide in my nose. I recoil slightly and drop my hand to the afghan. It makes a light thud that's so much more solid than Gemma's figure.

"I don't have much time," she whispers. "I'm ssstuck in a terrible, dark place." Her s's hiss in an ominous way that sound nothing like the Gemma I knew. "Sssomehow I broke free, but I feel its pull. It won't let me ssstay long." Her ghostly head darts back and forth as if looking for lurking evil.

Hot tears prick the corner of my eyes. When Gemma died, I went from doubting if there was an afterlife to imagining a beautiful one for my sister. This revelation of a dark place for her soul, the fear so clear on her face, is unbearable. I don't understand how she ended up anywhere other than paradise. She was always the kinder, more thoughtful one of the two of us, the angel on my devil shoulder.

I remind myself that I can't trust this. It may not be a dream, but that doesn't mean it isn't in my head.

She moves as if to stand. Despite my doubt in her realness, I reach out. "Wait!"

She shines bright for a moment and fades back to translucent. "Oh," she breathes. "Your love. That's what's allowing me to be here." Her expression is wary, closed in a way it never was in life. She leans in, her festering scent palpable. "It wasn't a missstake."

My brow wrinkles. "What wasn't a mistake?"

"My death."

Gemma's official cause of death was interstitial pneumonia of unknown causes, which is a bullshit way to say her lungs failed but the doctors couldn't figure out why. Neither could the Centers for Disease Control when her case was sent there, and that's basically all they do. She was classified as a medical mystery.

But I suddenly recall a conversation I overheard between the pathologist who performed my sister's autopsy and one of her colleagues. She said Gemma's lungs were so full of lesions, it looked like Gemma was poisoned. Is it possible *that* was the true cause of her death?

"No!" I clasp my hand over my mouth as what little I ate for dinner threatens to come back up.

It's not possible. No one wanted Gemma dead. Everyone loved her. At least they acted that way when she was alive. But maybe not everyone felt that way. If Camille —the person who claimed to be her best friend—loved her, then why did she start hooking up with Gemma's boyfriend, Logan, two weeks after her death?

But poison? Not possible. Because of the mysterious circumstances of Gemma's brief illness and death, a very thorough autopsy was performed. The toxicology reports said nothing about poison. My parents hired lawyers we couldn't afford to consider Gemma's case. There was no negligence or any reason to believe it wasn't a rare and tragic death of mysterious causes, not foul play.

I look over at this ghostly figure on my sister's bed, inhale the rottenness of it. This can't possibly be Gemma's spirit. It's a nightmare come to drive me insane with lies. It's grief-induced paranoia, the usual storm manifesting into this sinister hallucination.

I slip off the bed and back up until I hit my sister's dresser, her knickknacks rattling in protest. "No, no, no. Go away. You're not real."

"Delta, pleassse." Her mouth is open in shock, covered by her see-through hands. Translucent tears fall down her cheeks, and she promptly wipes them away, as if that's possible. Her eyes, which were once a deep brown, are all grayed out like the rest of her; they pin me with a steadfast gaze. "Delta, I know it doesn't make sense. Please lisssten."

She sounds a little more like herself and I inch closer, despite the goose bumps peppering my skin.

"Then we can play the quiet game," she says. "And I swear I won't lose tonight."

When Gemma and I were little, she used to have the hardest time falling asleep. Inevitably, as I would be dozing off, she would have one more question or story to tell. It used to drive me nuts. Then one day I challenged her to the quiet game. First one to speak would lose. She always lost, but usually, she would hold off long enough until I was asleep. Then she would confess to me in the morning. We hadn't played that game in years, and no one else knows about it.

That doesn't mean I'm not hallucinating, but at least I don't think she's some kind of impostor. I suppose there's no harm in hearing her out, maybe I just need to get this out of my system. I sit back down on the edge of the bed.

"Beware the ssstorm—" That's as far as she gets before her eyes go wide and her mouth opens in a silent scream.

Chapter 4

Gemma's ghostly form swirls into a ball of light before getting sucked into darkness. A pressure builds in the room and my ears pop like I'm on an airplane that's begun its descent.

My twin-not-twin is once again gone.

When the shock of having my sister's ghost visit me wears off, I'm left sitting on her bed in a dark room, my cheeks wet from tears. I wipe my face, take a deep breath, and hear the last words she said to me.

Beware the storm.

What the hell does that mean? Is it a metaphor? Gemma was the poet of the family and could spin a good metaphor. But without more information, it's impossible to know what she meant.

I fumble my way through the dark to my nightstand. It's way too late—or really too early—to call Emberly. With shaking hands, I pick up my phone and settle for a text.

> Something weird just
> happened...can't sleep

At the risk of seeming needy, I add a second message.

> Call me when you get this

Phone in hand, I pace the room, my head spinning and my body buzzing. The storm inside is churning up again like when Gemma first died. My breath comes in short gasps, like all the air is stuck inside me and there isn't enough outside of me to breathe properly.

When the dizziness makes it hard to stand, I fall onto my back on Gemma's bed. The scent of her pillow wafts up as my head hits it, not quite masking the stench of decay left behind by her ghost—or whatever that thing was. Can a hallucination leave behind a scent?

It's hard to trust anything right now, so I pinch my forearm again. A zip of pain shoots up my arm. Still awake.

My phone vibrates, and I bolt upright to answer it.

"Emberly." It comes out too breathy, and I sound like a ghost version of myself.

"You okay?" she asks, the urgency almost masking the sleepiness in her voice.

My heart rate jacks up at hearing her, as it always does, but in a good way. I imagine being next to her in bed and listening to her whisper in my ear.

"Delta, you there?" Emberly asks, sounding panicky.

The question brings me back to the reality of being in my sister's bed, not Emberly's, and what happened. "Yeah. I think…"

I lose my nerve and decide to keep quiet about the ghostly visit. Our relationship is new enough that I'm not sure how she'll respond. She's been amazing through my living nightmare of a summer—the extreme sadness, the panic attacks—but this latest thing is on a whole new level. She'll think I've gone mad.

"Nervous about seeing everyone again?" Emberly asks in a calmer voice.

Now I imagine her sitting up in bed, her face lit up eerily by the light of the phone. It's all ghosts in my head tonight. Ever since the funeral, I've been having a hard time being around large groups of people without panicking. The approaching school year has brought with it a whole slew of worries and stress.

"Yeah." It's not a lie, but it's also not the whole truth.

"Remember what your therapist said," Emberly reminds me.

After a couple of panic attacks, I saw a therapist for a few sessions. She gave me strategies for dealing with them and encouraged me to share the strategies with someone I trust, a person who can remind me of what to do when I feel an attack coming on. Emberly and I barely knew each other, but for some reason, I felt comfortable sharing with her. The sessions seemed to be working, but then I saw an unpaid bill on my mom's nightstand. The number on it convinced me I was cured, and I told my mom I didn't need to go anymore.

Emberly has been so amazingly supportive throughout this whole thing. I have no idea why; she hasn't known me long enough to feel it's an obligation. I haven't thought too deeply about it for fear of losing the only support system I have.

"One day at a time," I recite.

Tomorrow at school, I'll be the girl with the dead sister, instead of all those other things I used to be. That's what everyone is going to think about when they see me. That's all I'm going to think about when I see them. No one knows how to have a normal conversation with the sister of a dead girl.

Plus Camille will be there. I've managed to avoid her since I found out she's hooking up with Logan, but there will be no avoiding her once school starts, even with her being a senior and me being a junior. We have all the same friends.

Plus there's the swim team. If I want to be a supportive girlfriend that means showing up for meets, and that means seeing Camille.

I'm practically hyperventilating when Emberly's voice comes through the phone. "Deep breaths, Delta. Deep breaths." She does one herself as she says, "In and out...in and out."

Her coaching works, and I find a calmer rhythm. I'm such a mess, and I haven't even told her about the ghost.

Emberly proceeds to distract me by chatting about our classes and wondering who will be in them this year. She only knows a handful of kids from school, so it'll be a big adjustment for her too.

"Thanks, Em," I say through a yawn. It's after 2:00 a.m. now and I think I might actually be able to get some sleep before my alarm rings in a few hours.

"I'm sorry you're having a hard night." Having Emberly apologize when I'm the one who texted her in the middle of the night is one more reminder of how lucky I am to have her.

There's a lump in my throat when I say, "It's fine. I'm sorry I made you worry."

"Pick you up at seven?" she asks.

Emberly has her own car, so I can roll out of bed at 6:50 and be ready in time for her to drive me to school. Even when Gemma got her license, we didn't have a car, so we took the bus. I was supposed to take my driving test this summer, but those plans got derailed, so I only have a permit.

So many things are not how I expected them to be this year, and even a good thing of having a ride to school is tainted with grief. I'm learning that's the way life is: a big pile of bittersweet. Though I'm having trouble seeing the sweet.

"Good night, Delta."

"Night, Em."

The light goes off on my phone, leaving me in darkness. I finally fall asleep, still in my sister's bed, the sweet honeysuckle and sharp chlorine mixed in with the rot of death.

Chapter 5

By the time Emberly arrives to pick me up, the encounter with Gemma's ghost feels like a fever dream. I'm wondering if it really happened or if I imagined it. I don't mention it to Emberly. Last night would have been the time to do it, and now it feels too late.

After she parks in the student lot, Emberly rubs the woven bracelet she's always wearing. This one is red and navy blue, not the plain black one I'm used to seeing.

"New bracelet?" I ask. She nods, looking as nervous as I feel. "New school, new colors?"

"Something like that."

We sit in the car in tense silence, each one of us in our feelings and neither of us making a move to head out. I stare out the window at the students streaming by and listen to Emberly take a deep breath in and out. She reaches across the center console and caresses my hand, which is white-knuckled as I clutch the strap of my backpack in my lap.

Her deep brown eyes take in my face as I clench my jaw. "We got this."

I fake a smile. "Yeah. We got this."

Then it's out of the car and into the shark-infested waters of high school.

I squint in the bright morning sun. Heat emanates from the asphalt and it's not even 7:30. Summer break was brutally hot, and Emberly and I spent as much time as we could at the beach, the quiet one near her house so we wouldn't run into a million people. Feels like September is bringing more of the same heat. My scalp prickles with the humidity, and I'm happy that our school is air-conditioned.

But it's more than the stifling air that's making me feel like I can't breathe. It's the looming brick building in front of me, and the crowd of students milling in front of the entrance, taking their last sips of coffee and chatting about their summers.

People I know but wouldn't necessarily call friends say hello to Emberly and me. Some of them give me that look I know all too well—the one that says they're thinking about how I'm the dead girl's sister—and others don't quite make eye contact because they must pity me too much to look me straight on, like grief is catching.

I'm tempted to grab Emberly's hand, but mine is all sweaty. Plus, we've mostly hung out just the two of us or occasionally with Jasmine, so we haven't really tested the waters on public displays of affection.

I spot Jasmine before she sees me. She's leaning up against the wall near the door, one of her purple high-top sneakers propped up against the bricks. The reason why she can't see me is because she's currently lip-locked with Parker, the latest love of her life. We'll see how long that lasts. Parker's friend Briggs is the third-wheel next to them. I almost feel sorry for him, but he's kind of an arrogant prick, and Parker acts nicer when they aren't around Briggs.

Jasmine's lips break away from Parker's. When she spots me, she immediately slips out from under their arm and runs to me, her braids bouncing gently with her strides. She practically tackle-hugs me and then kisses my cheek in a strictly platonic way.

Our relationship is a fierce friendship, loyal and protective of each other. We were the same way with

Gemma and Camille. Then my sister died and Camille started hooking up with Logan, and now Jasmine and I are a sad twosome.

"Are you okay?" Jasmine's concern is not the same as the pity I get from everyone else. She's grieving, too, and it's like she's asking for herself as much for me.

I shrug and take a deep breath before speaking so my voice doesn't wobble. "I'm here."

"Yeah." Jasmine squeezes my shoulder. "You're here." Then she greets Emberly with a slightly less enthusiastic hug.

There's no sign of Camille. I try not to think about how that traitor is the one who introduced me to Emberly. It was at Briggs's end-of-year party, the one right before Gemma got sick. There were immediate sparks between us, but I had to leave early because Gemma and Logan got in a fight.

The next time I saw Emberly was at Gemma's wake. I had bailed on the never-ending receiving line, my internal storm churning so furiously, I couldn't breathe. She found me gasping behind a big oak tree and helped me calm down. It would have been one of the most embarrassing moments of my life if Emberly hadn't been so sweet. Her steadfastness in the storm of Gemma dying has been the only thing keeping me afloat.

Beware the storm.

Goose bumps rise up under the sweat on my arms as I think of ghostly Gemma's last words.

A stab of guilt runs through me as I realize that so much of my and Emberly's relationship has centered around my grief. My back-to-school anxiety has totally overshadowed the fact that this is her first day at a new school. I take a breath and try to bring myself back to the present.

Unaware—or perhaps ignoring—my maudlin mood, Emberly and Jasmine casually chat as we walk into the school and down the hallway where all upperclassmen have their lockers. Somewhere along the way, Parker joins us.

The memories have kept me from obsessing over whether everyone is looking at me.

Until Camille comes striding down the hallway with Logan by her side. His arm is slung around her shoulder and she's staring at him like she's never seen anything so captivating in her life.

I stop dead in the middle of the hallway, causing a backup as people bump into me from behind.

Jasmine grabs my hand on one side and Emberly puts a steadying arm around my waist. The three of us are blocking the entire hallway and it's causing a scene. A shout of "what's going on?" comes from somewhere.

As the traitorous couple gets closer, my vision turns dark around the edges.

"Breathe," Emberly whispers in my ear.

I loudly suck in a breath, but it doesn't clear away the darkness creeping at the edges. Camille and Logan pause when they reach us.

Logan nods. "Delta." It sounds husky with emotion, as if I remind him of my sister. But he has no right to feel any sort of way about my sister anymore.

Camille narrows her eyes for a second—so quickly I almost miss it—before her gaze slides away from me.

A sob threatens to rip through me. I break free from Emberly and Jasmine and run to the nearest bathroom.

Chapter 6

Hidden away in a bathroom stall, instead of the good cry I was anticipating having, I succumb to a panic attack. Cotton fills my throat and my heart beats faster than when I almost drowned.

My breaths come hard and fast, but I'm not taking in enough air. On my knees, I grip the edges of the toilet seat but barely feel the cool edges biting into my skin as my muscles lock up.

I try to remember my strategies, but the ringing in my ears is taking up all the space in my brain. A door slams. There's a knock like from the end of a tunnel and the stall door shakes behind me.

"Delta! Remember, deep belly breaths." Emberly's voice has been pulling me out of panic attacks all summer, but it's not working this time. I'm caught up in the squeeze of anxiety.

There's more banging on the door...and voices, but they sound so far away. I can't make sense of them. Then Jasmine appears as if from out of nowhere, a magician doing an appearance act, the whites of her eyes large with fear.

"What do I have her do?" she shouts at the door. She's so close in the tiny bathroom stall. Her words are too loud, tightening the vice on my body.

I lose track of what's going on as my vision tunnels. I think I'm going to pass out, but then the scratch of a dry hand on mine brings me back to my body. The hand guides mine to my stomach and holds it there.

"Delta!" Jasmine's face is right in front of me. I focus on her lips, her top one glistening with sweat. "Belly breaths."

Our hands push gently on my stomach as Jasmine demonstrates with her own deep breath, Emberly coaching her on what to do from the other side of the door. My breath follows Jasmine's, a fresh burst of air filling me in a heady but deeply satisfying way.

"That's it," Jasmine says. "Keep breathing." Our hands continue moving on my stomach in time with our breaths. The black recedes from my vision and the bathroom stall suddenly feels too bright, the metal door cold against my back.

I take in the whole of Jasmine's face, staring at me with worried eyes, a deep crease in her forehead.

"You okay?" she asks.

My mouth is dry like sand after a windstorm, so I nod, unable to find my voice. My body is sore and sweaty, but the vice has loosened.

Jasmine pulls her rough hand—she complains that there's not enough lotion on God's green earth to keep her skin moisturized during swim season—from mine and squeezes my upper arms, steadying me.

"Can I hug you?" she asks.

I hold my finger up so she'll give me a moment. Then the tears I thought were coming in the hallway finally break through. I nod and fall into her, my tears soaking her shoulder. She holds me until the tears subside.

"How did you get in here?" I ask.

"I climbed under."

The space under stall walls is tiny, and a smile comes to my face as I picture Jasmine squeezing underneath, coming to my rescue. Our eyes meet and there's a smile on her face, too.

She touches her forehead to mine. "Only for you would I touch that nasty floor."

Then we crack up, our laughter echoing in that unique public restroom way. It lightens me as only a best friend can do.

Another knock comes from outside the stall, gentle this time. "Can I come in?" Emberly asks in a timid voice.

I manage a croaky "yes." Jasmine reaches behind me and turns the lock. Then I'm sandwiched between the two of them in a sweaty embrace, my best friend in front of me and my girlfriend behind. My two anchors in the storm of Gemma's death.

My momentary peace is disturbed when images of ghostly Gemma surface. I shiver despite the warm bodies pressing in on me. If she was right, I'm in for a second storm. I'm barely surviving this one, so I don't know how I'll get through another, solid anchors or not.

Chapter 7

After the confrontation with Camille and Logan and the panic attack, it's hard to concentrate in my classes. I used to be good at school, but ever since Gemma died, it's like I don't know myself anymore. That was "before Delta" who was good at school. What is this "after Delta" like? She doesn't feel good at anything; she can barely make her way through the day.

When last period finally rolls around, I stop short in the doorway of my history class. Logan sits in the back of the room. Perched on his desk is none other than the worst-best-friend-to-a-dead-sister Camille.

I haven't seen her since the incident in the hallway, and I guess I'm not lucky enough to have avoided her all day. Neither Emberly nor Jasmine are in this class, so there's no one here to remind me to breathe.

I kind of don't care that I probably look like a weirdo when I put my hand on my belly and feel it move up and down with a deep breath. I imagine Emberly's soft voice slowly telling me "in and out," and that helps. Then I sit in the very front of the room as far away from the traitors as I can.

Mr. Richards, who so far had been ignoring the murmurs and chatter of the class, calls us to attention as the bell rings. He takes attendance, briefly pausing at my name but thankfully not acknowledging me in any other way.

He moves on from roll call to an overview of class. "We'll cover the pre-Columbian era all the way to today.

That's a lot of history to cover in less than 180 days." He pauses and gives a loud chuckle, like he made the funniest joke in the history of the world. No one so much as cracks a smile, so he plunges back into his speech, moving on to what to expect when it comes time for the AP exam.

A headache is creeping from my temples to the top of my head and my muscles are achy, so I'm finding it hard to concentrate. The therapist explained that panic attacks can take a lot out of you, both physically and mentally, and to take it easy on myself when I've had one. But it's not like I could have bailed on the entire first day of school.

This year is supposed to set me up for college. Junior year grades are the ones all the schools will weigh the most on applications. I can't afford to fuck it up, but all I want to do is go home and cry into my pillow until I fall asleep.

I prop my head up with my hand and manage to stay awake until the last bell rings. I shut my laptop harder than necessary, sling my bag over my shoulder, and hightail it out of there without a backward glance at Camille and Logan.

Since Emberly has swim practice after school, I'm reduced to taking the bus home. The last two years I've run cross country, but I didn't sign up for any fall sports or activities. Simply going to school is enough for right now. I've been running on my own when I feel up to it, which admittedly isn't very often.

I joined the cross country team my freshman year to avoid coming home to an empty house. When Gemma and I were younger, we had each other. Then Gemma got serious about swimming. When she started high school, I suddenly had a lot of alone time at home and never did quite get used to the feel of an empty house. Now it always feels like it's empty, even when my parents are there.

Today, though, my mom is home. She's in her room packing, a 24-hours news channel on in the background.

"Delta!" she says a little too enthusiastically when I poke my head in. "How was the first day?"

I shrug. "Fine." No need to worry her about my problems; she's got enough of her own.

In a nasally voice that sets my teeth on edge, a guy on TV drones on about a tropical storm turning into a hurricane off the coast of the Bahamas.

I nod toward the TV. "Is that going to affect your trip?" My parents were gifted an all-expense paid trip to Jamaica after Gemma died. An anonymous donor paid for it and set up the whole thing, as if sitting on a tropical beach sipping a Mai Tai makes you feel better about your dead daughter.

She doesn't bother looking up from the mound of clothes on the bed. "Tropical Storm Ophelia? No, it's north of Jamaica and is supposed to head out to sea." She looks up in the middle of folding a long, flowing skirt. "Are you worried? Should Gary and I stay home?"

"No, Mom." I roll my eyes. We've been over this a million times. "Go on your trip. I'll be fine."

I have zero confidence that I've been anywhere near fine in the last two months, but keeping my parents from going to Jamaica isn't going to change that. Normally my mom wouldn't be able to take ten days off from work, and my parents certainly wouldn't have been able to afford this trip on their own. But they're still in the honeymoon phase of having a dead daughter, so everyone is making exceptions for them.

It's not that I'm not mad about my parents being the benefactor of people's misguided kindness. If anyone deserves a vacation, it's them. I'm angry that they only have this opportunity because tragedy struck our family. Everyone deserves to have a nice vacation while their kid is alive.

My mom's giving me a look like she's not sure she should go.

"Seriously," I say. "Jasmine's gonna stay here this weekend," and probably Emberly, but I don't say that because I'm pretty sure she doesn't want to hear about my girlfriend staying overnight, "and I'll be busy with school the rest of the time."

"Okay, okay." Her eyes are misty—I don't know how she has any tears left in her, honestly—and pulls me in for a hug. "You call Grandma if you need anything. She'll drive right down here."

My grandmother, my mom's mom, is the only grandmother I've ever known because my dad walked out on us when Gemma and I were little and Gary's parents died before he met my mom. She lives a few hours away in Massachusetts. She doesn't drive very well during the day and not at all at night, so there's zero chance I'll call her. As long as I have Jasmine and Emberly, I'll be okay.

My mom goes back to packing, and I head to my room. When I get there, I pull up short of entering. The distraction of the first day of school and my parents' trip has kept Gemma's ghostly visit in the back of my mind. Now that I'm here in our room, the scene is fresh...and still confounding.

Rather than think about it, I throw on my running clothes and sneakers and head out into the heat of late afternoon. There's little chance of me outrunning the thoughts cycling through my head, but maybe I can get my body tired enough to sleep tonight without any visitors.

Chapter 8

Running helps me exactly zero percent. With the heat outside and the increased muscle soreness, it's making me feel worse.

A headache pulses at my temples as I peel off my sweaty clothes and take a legit cold shower, another indicator of my questionable mental state. Once I'm shivering, I switch on the hot water and let the spray wash over me until the entire shower fills with steam.

With Gemma gone, there's no one to care how long I take in the shower anymore since my parents have a separate one. Two bathrooms is one of the only good things about our tiny two-bedroom house. I used to hate sharing a room. Now it feels perpetually lonely in there; the world feels perpetually lonely without Gemma.

Once I've had my fill of hot water, I get out of the shower and wrap one towel around my body and another around my hair. Using two towels is a luxury I'd gladly give up if it meant having to share with Gemma.

The mirror is so steamed up, it's dripping in some places. I wipe a circle clean and find a tired face in the reflection. Dark circles and poor bathroom lighting suck the life out of my face. As the circle begins to fill back in with fog, a flash of movement in the mirror catches my eye.

I whip around, my heart racing, my body filling with heat. It makes me lightheaded, and I'm afraid I might pass out. I sit on the closed toilet and put my head between my legs, the towel falling off my hair. The wave of dizziness passes, but the steamy conditions remain.

The mist in the air swirls around in an unnatural pattern. It coalesces into a form I know, but one I'm not sure I want to see. Not with the uncertainty of knowing if it's really Gemma and the disturbing ideas she's put in my head.

The same stench of rot from the other night overtakes the scent of my coconut shampoo. Gemma's ghostly mouth twists into a grimace, like she wants to speak but can't. Even with my doubts about the reality of what's happening, her expression pulls at my darkest emotions, churning up the storm in my belly.

Her ghostly form swirls with the mist in a way that distorts her image. Her mouth gapes open, a fish out of water. No speech comes.

"Gemma, I have to know." There's a desperate plea to my voice. "Did Camille poison you?"

"Beware the ssstorm." It's that hissing voice that sounds nothing like my sister.

"What storm?" I shiver, the temperature in the bathroom suddenly cold, despite the steam.

Her eyes are wide, the whites translucent, and every detail of the seashell shower curtain behind her shows through. She opens her mouth, but she's struck mute again. Her form lurches backward as if something invisible is pulling on it. Her body wrenches back and forth, part of it disappearing altogether at times. Her head whips back and forth.

"Gemma!" My shriek is desperate, my heart despairing.

The struggle that I can only half-see continues, her body pulling against an unseen foe.

I stand, clutching the towel to my chest, and reach for her. "Tell me something…anything."

"Beware the ssstorm," she manages in a voice barely there.

Then she's gone again. The temperature in the bathroom instantly warms.

I fall to my knees and sob into my towel. Every time she leaves, it punches a new hole through my chest. Pretty soon I'll be nothing more than a thin outline around gaping cavities filled with the raging winds of grief. My chest heaves, a final sob echoing off the bathroom walls.

The mist disappeared with Gemma. The bathroom mirror is clear except for one spot in the corner, big enough for someone to have written in the condensation.

Beware the storm.

That damn message with no more explanation than before. No answer to my question about Camille. No sense of relief at having connected with my dead sister. Just this angry, swirling storm twisting my insides.

I grab the towel off the floor and wipe away the fading words with one angry swipe at the mirror.

Chapter 9

I've never really thought much about the expression "sleep like the dead." I always thought it meant you slept so well it was like you were dead. So that would mean you'd wake up refreshed.

But dead people don't wake up, unless you count the appearance of Gemma's ghost as waking up. Wherever she comes from seems more like a nightmare. If the dead people who wake up come from a terrible place, then the expression makes no sense at all.

So I guess it's safe to say that I slept like the dead because I feel like the waking dead in the morning.

My parents are gone when I go down to grab a banana for breakfast. A car came very early this morning to bring them to the airport for their flight to Jamaica. We said our goodbyes last night, my mom getting all weepy over leaving me. Everything makes her weepy lately.

I lock the quiet tomb of my house behind me when Emberly arrives.

"Morning." She greets me with a smile when I fumble my way into the passenger seat.

We're not the PDA type, mostly because that's just not who we are but also a little bit because some people can be weird about two girls kissing. Aside from a few kisses at the beach, Emberly and I haven't really been all that physical since we've been together. I've been so consumed with grief, it hasn't left much room for other feelings.

I've gotten used to a light peck on the lips as a greeting when we're alone. But this time when our lips meet over the center console, I hesitate to pull away. Emberly pulls back just a little, a question in the tilt of her eyebrows.

I lean farther in and gently place my hand on the back of her head, her hair soft and a touch damp from her morning shower. We stare into each other's eyes for a moment before our lips meet again.

I let myself linger over their softness and take in the tropical scent of her damp hair, a hint of chlorine behind it. This summer it was all suntan lotion and salt water smells between us, and I like discovering a new scent of hers. It means we've been together long enough to really start getting to know one another.

It's not long before our lips pressing together isn't enough. I part mine to take her bottom lip into my mouth. My hand presses more firmly to the back of her head, and her hands find my hips somehow, even with the console between us. Our kiss deepens, and she teases my lips with her tongue before pressing all the way in.

Our stolen moments at the beach are nothing compared to this. This summer was more about connecting mentally rather than physically, which is what I think we both needed. I was trying to figure out my new sisterless self, and she was trying to figure out her place in a new town

There's an urgency to this kiss that hasn't been there before, like it's a precursor to something more.

A little anger, sadness, and frustration eke out of me with each movement of her lips and tongue against mine. It's the release I sought during my run that never came, and now I've found it with Emberly. All kinds of new feelings are stirring up inside me.

I've always liked Emberly since that first spark at the

end-of-school party. We found ourselves alone in the hot tub after Jasmine and Camille had made a not-so-subtle exit. At some point Gemma and Logan had a big fight, so Jasmine was back before Emberly and I had a chance to do more than chitchat in the way you do with a person you could like but just met.

Because of the nature of our second meeting at my sister's wake, our relationship took a serious turn when it was just getting started. With so much grief in my heart, it was hard to let anything else in. Without having to say anything, we both knew we needed to take it slow. Our relationship up until now has been very friendship-like, a slow discovery of each other, that first spark there but in the backseat.

I was okay with that, more than okay with it. We were giving each other what we needed; we were being careful, with ourselves and each other. Who knew a spontaneous kiss would shift that?

When we finally come up for air, the world is brighter. My head is full of Emberly, but it's never felt lighter. We stare at each other sheepishly but not embarrassed, Emberly absentmindedly rubbing her red and navy blue bracelet.

"We should get to school," she says like she's trying to convince herself.

I nod, though all I want to do is invite her into my empty house, take her up to my bedroom, and see where that kiss leads us.

I clear my throat, but my voice sounds husky when I say, "We wouldn't want to be late on our second day."

Emberly bites her bottom lip, which I can't stop staring at, and shifts the car into drive. It's been running this whole time, but I barely noticed. As she drives, I roll down the window to try and cool my cheeks. I stick my hand outside the window and let it ride the air current, a secret smile on my lips.

I feel like I left behind a whole other self the moment I shut the car door. A piece of me that I lost when Gemma died has filled in. Not replacing her—nothing could ever do that—but calming the perpetual storm and putting something soothing in its place.

The name for it comes to me as we arrive at school. It's love, that's what might finally temper the storm. And it's Emberly that made me see that...made me start to feel that. I wouldn't say I'm in love with Emberly, but for the first time in months, the potential to feel something other than grief is there.

One of my anchors has now become a sail, if only I'm brave enough to fill it with air.

Chapter 10

I ride the wave of our heated kiss all the way through the day. It's not until I reach AP history that reality comes crashing back to me. One glance at Camille's pouty face brings back the latest visit from Gemma's ghost and all my questions burning for answers.

Camille's sitting next to Logan but staring straight ahead as if he doesn't exist. Logan keeps sneaking glances at her, but she's having none of it. Guess she's mad at him, and my uncharitable heart hopes it's ripping them apart.

I consider straight up asking them if they had anything to do with Gemma's death. Or at the very least fishing around to see if they knew anything about her death that they haven't told anyone.

Because of the unknown nature of Gemma's illness and cause of death, all of us—her family, friends, teammates—got asked a lot of questions. The expert doctors the lawyer hired in particular wanted to know all about the last few days before she got sick as they tried to figure out what caused her death.

I went over in detail the end-of-school party at Briggs' house.

The doctors—and later the lawyers—asked me all about what Gemma drank that night, if she did any drugs, who she was in contact with. Most of it I couldn't answer because I was with Emberly in the hot tub.

But I've gone over and over that night in my head.

We weren't there that long because of Gemma and Logan's fight. Jasmine, Gemma, and I huddled in the bed of

Logan's old pickup truck, ducking down to stay out of sight of other cars, and Camille in the cab with Logan. She later claimed it was because Gemma didn't want to sit near him, but I've been wondering if there was something already happening between those two. Maybe that's why Gemma was mad.

I remember the warmth of Gemma's shoulder against mine. Except for the rush of wind, it was silent until music came blaring from the cab. Gemma half-heartedly sang along, her perfect pitch a contrast to my off-key one.

Later that night in our room, Gemma said she was too tired to talk about it and went straight to sleep. I didn't push her for more information, thinking she would talk when she was ready or the whole thing would blow over.

The next morning Gemma stayed in bed because she felt like she was coming down with something. When Monday rolled around, she'd hardly left her bed and had a bad cough, so she stayed home from school. Then Tuesday came and she wasn't feeling better, so my mom took her to the doctor's.

He thought it was pneumonia and prescribed her an antibiotic, rest, and lots of fluids. By the next weekend, she wasn't any better, worse actually. That's when they admitted her to Regional General hospital. It happens to be one of the best hospitals in the country, but that didn't matter. Gemma got sicker and sicker until they couldn't do anything for her. It was less than three weeks from that party to when she died.

If I had known it was going to be the last party with Gemma, I would've done so many things differently. Though, I'm not sure I would have wanted to know it was the one because it would have been impossible to enjoy it. You hear that saying about living in the moment because you never know when it will be your last, but I think it's just as important to do that in case it's the last moments of someone you love.

I would've stayed by Gemma's side. I would've known what she drank, if she smoked, what the fight was about. I would've been there to watch out for my twin-not-twin. If Camille and Logan did do something to her at the party, I would have been there. Maybe to stop it, maybe not. Either way, I would've been there. But I wasn't.

In class, Mr. Richards drones on while I ruminate over all of this, unable to decide if I'm going to confront Camille and Logan.

In the end, I chicken out and bolt out of class to catch my bus. I torture myself over my cowardice. As the bus passes the beach, I stare at the water, the reflected sunlight bringing tears to my eyes. At least that's what I tell myself the tears are from.

A text comes in from Jasmine just before my stop.

Party this weekend. Sea Glass Lodge.

The Sea Glass Lodge is an old abandoned beach house that sits all by itself at the end of a long, winding road. Thinking about going to a party there makes my palms sweat. Parties are my worse nightmare...well, aside from the whole being haunted by my dead sister thing.

I race off the bus and try not to hyperventilate as I walk the block to my house. If just thinking about a party—all those people, their pitying eyes and awkward side glances—pushes me toward a panic attack, imagine what an actual party will do.

The three dots sit under her message, which means she's probably waiting for a response. I want to text back "hell no," but I also know I've been a shitty friend all summer.

Jasmine loves parties, and I used to love them, too, when it was the inseparable foursome all together. All summer long, Jasmine went out without me. I didn't even know she was dating Parker until two weeks after they first hooked up at the 4th of July fireworks.

Emberly and I spent that night at the end of the rock jetty at the private beach near her house, watching the fireworks show from afar. All the smaller ones people were setting off along the coastline added to the big bursts of light. We kissed a little, but my favorite thing was sitting there next to her, resting my head on her shoulder, our hands entwined between us.

Jasmine claimed she needed to blow off steam this summer, so she partied every opportunity she got. I totally understand her needs were different than mine, but it meant we were apart more than we were together for the first time in many summers.

Neither of us has said anything out loud about it, but the underlying rift is there. With the start of school, I think she was hoping things would go back to normal.

The problem is that I don't know what the hell normal is anymore.

I don't want to drift apart from my best friend. She's been hurting all summer, too, even if she's dealt with it in a very different way than I have. I can't let the fact that Emberly has been here for me in a way Jasmine hasn't take the place of what I have with my best friend. A girlfriend is not a best friend.

By the time I calm down and settle in my room with a glass of water in my shaking hands, the three dots are gone from the message. Swim practice must have started, so that gives me time to answer.

Instead of obsessing over the fact that Camille is there with Jasmine and Emberly, I picture Emberly in her bathing suit. Not her practice suit, which is a boring navy blue one-piece. She has this bright orange bikini she wore all summer long. I love teasing her that she would never get lost at sea in that thing. She looks gorgeous in it, her sun-kissed skin barely covered.

My imagination turns on me when Emberly's face turns into Camille's, my girlfriend's long dark hair morphing into my enemy's blond curls. Then my brain imagines Logan appearing at the beach near Emberly's house. He's kissing Emberly-turned-Camille, his hands all tangled up in her hair. Far out on the same rock jetty where Emberly and I watched the fireworks, stands Gemma's ghost. Her mouth is open in a silent scream. Behind her the water is calm, until a rogue wave crashes over the rocks, pulling her out to sea. Camille and Logan stop kissing long enough to point and laugh at Gemma as she disappears under the water.

I wake with a start, the room quiet and dark. My phone blinks with unread messages. It's after eight, and I've been asleep for a good four hours.

Yet, once again, I don't feel rested.

My mind is churning, and I would give nearly anything to turn it off.

I ignore the messages and decide to take a walk. It's only a half mile to the beach—the public one, not the nice one near Emberly's—but I can't stay in this deadly quiet house another minute.

Act II

"...to take arms against a sea of
troubles, and by opposing end them?"

William Shakespeare
Hamlet
Act III, Scene I

Chapter 11

The sun is below the houses as I walk through my neighborhood, but it hasn't fully set. I get to the beach in time to catch it sinking below the horizon of water. The sky flares up yellow before softening to a velvety purple. A bright star sits in the western sky, twinkling in the twilight.

The breeze off the water isn't what I would call cool, but it's refreshing. The stinging scent of saltiness is cleansing. A barefoot couple slowly strolls along where hard-packed sand meets water. A man briskly walks his dog up on the sidewalk near the street.

I take off my flip-flops, head to the water line, and let the warm shallows wash over my toes. I walk in the opposite direction as the couple, the wet sand squishing in a satisfying way between my toes.

Darkness continues to fall, cloaking me and all my misery. I once again wonder how different the first two days of school would have been if Gemma were here. What it would have been like to finally be in a class together. What she would've thought of Emberly. If we would've become the inseparable five with Logan in tow. Maybe Gemma and Emberly would be forming a friendship together, separate from the role of Emberly being my girlfriend. That would've been nice.

They probably would have found all kinds of things to tease me about, and it probably would've been only a little annoying. Definitely Emberly would be let in on the long-running jokes about my lack of swimming talent.

Our summer would have been different, too. Two whole months of parties and hanging out together. I would be looking forward to the first party of the school year, not dreading it.

We would be carefree.

Instead, I'm walking on the beach alone. Only one piece in the puzzle is missing, but it ruined the whole thing. Now it seems none of the pieces fit together anymore.

I flop down onto the ground, not caring that the water immediately soaks into my shorts. I rest my head back on the drier part of the sand. More stars pop out in the sky that grows ever darker.

I come back to the question that's been plaguing me all summer. A question that my time with Emberly can only stave off for a little while. As soon as I'm alone, I think about it.

How does a perfectly healthy 17-year-old suddenly get sick and die and no one can figure out why?

With the lack of answers, the other questions come. How did Camille and Logan think it would ever be okay for them to hook up mere weeks after my sister died? Will I ever be comfortable around big groups of people again? What is this world without my sister?

Then there are new questions brought about by Gemma's ghostly visits. Was Gemma poisoned? What is this storm she keeps talking about?

They're important questions, but none of them press down as hard as the most important one. And that question is the one I can't stop thinking about as the tide creeps up on me, soaking farther and farther up my body.

Do I want to exist in a world that doesn't hold Gemma?

There is so much pain here without her. Sure there

was pain before, but none like this, so persistent, so all-consuming. And any pain I did feel, I had Gemma there as a buffer.

Not that the afterlife seems to be shaping up to be so wonderful if Gemma's ghost is any indication. But who's to say that's really her—or whatever essence of her still remains. Maybe it's all in my head. Or maybe I want to think Gemma is in a "better place" in order to make myself feel better.

There could be nothing at all after this life.

But if this life is misery and pain, then nothingness might be a sweet respite.

I lay back and take in the sky. The moon has yet to make an appearance, so it's all stars in the vast expanse. Are there other worlds out there in the universe? Are they better than this one?

If there are, I guess it doesn't matter because I will never go to them.

The tide has reached my shoulders, the water warm, so it's not unpleasant. I'm perfectly comfortable here, soaking away, the salt seeping into my pores.

I could lay here, let the tide take me all the way in. I'd probably float for a while, not as long as Gemma could have with her superior swim skills. Eventually my body would tire, the muscles seizing up. I'd sink under the surface, hold my breath at first. Then my lungs would run out of air, just like Gemma's did.

I might panic, or maybe a calm would wash over me as I sank down, down, down. The first gulp of salt water would sting. But then I'd grow used to it. My lungs would fill with liquid, just like Gemma's did.

Would I feel my last breath or would I pass out first? Would I know when I slipped from one world to the other?

Or would I end up somewhere in between, like Gemma? If that ghost is really her.

The water reaches the back of my head. My hair undulates as the soft waves pull in and out along the water line. I close my eyes, feel the push and pull.

Just as the water reaches my ears, I hear someone call out in a frantic voice, "Gemma! Gemma!"

As the water mutes my sense of hearing, the call for my sister turns into my name.

"Delta!"

Chapter 12

I ignore the shouts—they're probably not real anyway—and luxuriate in a dance with the waves. The salty water reaches my lips, my nose barely poking out. I keep my eyes shut tight. I'm not scared of the water this time.

The higher the water rises, the calmer I become, the more I can sense myself getting closer to my sister. A little longer and I could be with her again if that's what I want.

Strong hands grasp my shoulders and yank me from my sweet reverie. They prop me up in a sitting position. The parts of my body no longer submerged in water instantly break out with goose bumps.

The calm vanishes, panic taking over. I gulp for air but can't find any. It's like the tide consumes me, only instead of drowning in water, I'm drowning in the never-ending storm of grief.

"Delta!" It's that same voice I heard before the water clogged my ears, clearer now so I recognize it.

That voice makes me angry enough to find my breath. I whip open my eyes. Logan's kneeling next to me, his face far too close to mine.

"What are you doing here?" I spit out.

"What am I doing here?" he asks in disbelief.

From behind me comes a mocking voice, "What are you doing here?"

The look I shoot at Parker and Briggs should kill them both straight dead. Maybe it's too dark for them to get the full force, but it's strong enough to send a message that gets them moving down the beach, Parker muttering, "We'll get the fire started."

"Seriously, Delta," Logan says. "Why were you in the water like that?"

"What do you care?" It comes out more defensive than I want it to.

"What the hell does that mean?" He looks genuinely hurt, his forehead scrunched up in an adorable way that reminds me that my sister loved this boy. "You're like a sister to me."

I want to spit at him for calling me that. "Gemma's funeral was barely over when you hooked up with Camille." I hate how my voice breaks over the traitor's name. "Did you ever love her?" We both know I mean Gemma.

"Of course." He slumps down next to me, and I feel like I can breathe better now that he's not in my face. "I loved her so much."

There are so many things I want to ask him, but my brain wars over where to start.

He doesn't wait for me to decide. "I get why you hate me. But the reason I'm with Camille," I growl because every time I hear that name the storm roils inside me, "isn't because I didn't love Gemma. It's because I loved her so much."

A noise that's a cross between a gag and throat clearing comes out of my mouth.

"I know," he says. "It sounds so stupid, and I'm the one saying it. Look, Gemma's death tore me up bad. Camille gets how that feels. It helps to be with someone who gets it. You know?"

I don't know because no one felt the way I did about Gemma. She wasn't just a girlfriend or a friend to me, she was my sister. My only one, and I was hers. In a lifetime, you might have dozens of romantic partners and friends, but I only got one sister. There will never be another.

He's staring at me while I try to figure out how to explain it to him. I realize I can't, so I settle on stony silence.

"When I first spotted you in the water like that," his Adam's apple bobbles as he swallows, "I thought you were Gemma. I was so happy for a second, until I realized it couldn't be her. Then when I realized it was you, it scared the hell out of me. You weren't trying to...?"

If he can't be brave enough to say exactly what he wants to ask me, I don't feel the need to answer him, but I also don't let up my stare.

"Will you ever be able to forgive us?" he asks, staring out at the water now. "I don't want to lose you forever, too."

He sounds so sincere that I want to believe him. I want to think that it was mutual grief that drove Logan and Camille together, however misguided. But I can't get the image of my sister's ghost out of my head. Her silent screams. Her hissing voice.

I tiptoe around the question I wanted to ask him and Camille earlier in AP history. "Do you ever wonder if it wasn't a random sickness that killed Gemma? If maybe it was something else?"

Logan jerks his gaze away from the water and back to me, like my question pulled his thoughts from far away. "Something else? Like what? I thought it was declared a medical mystery."

"What if it wasn't a freak illness?" I muse. "What if it was done on purpose?"

Logan's mouth gapes open, shock in his wide eyes. "Like she did it to herself?"

"No." The word is laced with poison. "Murder."

"Who would want to murder Gemma?"

I want to believe his incredulity, but it's hard for me to believe anyone right now. "Someone could have wanted to."

"Did one of the doctors think that's what happened?" he says in a tortured whisper.

Tortured because the idea of Gemma being murdered tears him up or tortured because he's afraid of being found out?

I needle a little harder. "The pathologist who did the autopsy said something." I watch him very closely to see how he'll react to my next words. "She said Gemma's lungs were so messed up with scar tissue that it looked like someone had poisoned her."

Logan shivers, and I shiver along with him. It's only then that I remember that we're sitting waist deep in water. The water itself is warm, but the air has cooled and now I'm cold. My teeth begin to chatter and that seems to bring Logan back to reality.

"Shit!" he says. "Let's get you out of this water. Parker and Briggs have a fire going. Come warm up by it." He touches my elbow like he's going to help me up, but I lean away.

"I should go home." I stand on my own. My flip-flops are miraculously still looped through my fingers.

"You should stay and dry off. Then I'll give you a ride."

"I don't need a ride."

"Aren't your mom and stepdad on their trip?"

I didn't realize he knew my parents were gone. Who else has been keeping tabs on me? "Yeah, so what?" I have no patience left for Logan.

"Maybe you shouldn't be alone right now is all I'm saying. Gemma wouldn't want anything bad to happen to you.”

I hate the way he invokes my sister and what she would've wanted. I hate even more that he's right.

I'm not in a great place right now. It's a little scary to think about what I would have let happen if Logan hadn't found me in the water when he did.

"Fine." I concede. "I'll stay until I'm dry, but I don't need a ride home."

As if I don't care about anything, I flounce away to where a fire is now blazing not too far up the beach. The truth is I care about everything far too much, and it's making me more messed up than ever.

Chapter 13

I'm in a strange stand-off with Logan and his friends. They're on one side of the fire, drinking beer and being loud, and I'm on the other, trying to hide how much I'm shivering.

I down a beer quickly because it's something to do with my shaking hands, and it at least makes my belly warm.

Parker and Briggs are pretty much ignoring me, but I can't miss the worried glances Logan throws my way. He tosses an empty beer can into the fire and breaks the barrier between our sides.

He produces a joint from his pocket. "You want the first hit?"

"I don't smoke." Gemma, Jasmine, and Camille used to smoke once in a while, but it never appealed to me. I'll drink any random concoction people make for parties, but smoking has never been my thing.

"I know," Logan says. "It's just...you seem stressed out, and this might help."

He's not wrong. "Does it help you?"

"It does. Gives my brain a break from everything." He lights it up and hands it to me.

It seems wrong to put a thing in my mouth that was just in the mouth of a guy who's kissed my sister. A mouth that now kisses Camille. But if I've ever needed a break from my own thoughts now is the time.

I take the joint and suck in deep—too deep. I cough out smoke.

Parker and Briggs laugh and whoop. Logan reaches for a hit, but I hang on to it and take another. This time I know what to expect and hold it in for a moment before I smoothly exhale.

Logan smiles as I hand it to him, and I try not to think about Gemma talking to me in the dark of the night about all the things she loved about him. None of those things matter anymore now that he's with Camille, no matter what he says about it helping with his grief.

The joint gets passed around. I have every intention of sending it right on through to Logan when it comes back around, but I take a hit when Briggs holds it out. I'm not really feeling anything yet. I've heard you might not the first time you smoke, but I'd really like to experience some of that relief Logan was talking about.

It's getting late and it's a Tuesday night, so we're the only ones on the beach, until a group of three girls head our way from one of the beach paths. I don't need to look at them long to recognize Jasmine and Emberly. The third person I recognize as well, and the only place I want to see her in is hell.

Camille waves and runs the rest of the way to the fire, sand kicking up behind her.

"Logan!" she squeals as she throws herself at him. He hugs her, but he's watching me. Camille accepts the dwindling joint and takes a hit. If it lasts long enough to come back to me, I won't touch it.

My gaze locks on Logan's, and he has the sense to look awkward with Camille draped all over him. Earlier, Logan's surprise at my probing about Gemma's death seemed genuine. I'm not saying I trust him, but I definitely don't trust Camille. She offered her condolences to my family at the wake, but she's barely said a word to me since then. It's been all dodgy looks on her part and silent accusations on mine.

Arms wrap around me, and I recognize the woven bracelet enclosing a delicate wrist. I turn right into a kiss from Emberly. Instantly, I'm back in the car with her this morning, my hands and lips longing to explore her more.

"I've been texting and calling you." Her voice is gentle, more worried than mad.

"I forgot my phone at home."

She pecks me on the cheek. "I forgive you."

"I don't," says Jasmine. She has what is left of the joint hanging from her mouth, and Parker has an arm around her shoulder already.

"Shotgun?" Parker asks.

Jasmine takes a long drag and leans into Parker as they open their mouth, then she blows smoke into it. They finish it with a kiss that almost makes me blush.

Emberly gets the last hit of the joint, the embers so close to her fingers it must be burning them. I almost don't want to kiss her after having the Camille-tainted thing in her mouth—almost.

"We stopped by your house, Delta, because you weren't answering any of our messages," Jasmine says. "I got worried when no one was home."

The others have gone back to drinking beer, Camille joining them.

"I went for a walk and forgot my phone." I shrug. "Then I ran into these clowns and decided to stay." It's the truth, if not the whole truth.

Jasmine scrutinizes me with a look before giving me a hug. "I guess I can forgive you since you're actually partying tonight."

I am partying and I'm not super self-conscious about

being the girl with the dead sister. Though, I'm not without worries about what others are thinking; they're just not my usual worries.

"I'm glad, too." Emberly puts her arm around my waist and squeezes my hip. With her other hand, she touches my hair, which is a little crispy from the dried salt water. "Did you go swimming?"

"Delta, swimming?" Jasmine says. "No way. She hates swimming."

I roll my eyes at the old joke. "I can float just fine." And doggy paddle like it's nobody's business, but I'd never say that in front of all the superstar swimmers. "It was more wading than swimming."

I'm certainly not going to tell them how Logan found me in the water like a damsel in distress, minus the dragon. Or maybe the dragon was inside the damsel in this case. No that's wrong, too, because it's a storm, not a dragon, inside me. My thoughts are growing both fuzzy and outlandish.

I swing myself around, so I'm face-to-face with Emberly. Her eyes look very big tonight and her lips look very soft, kissable. I giggle.

"Did you smoke?" Jasmine asks. Apparently, she's full of questions with obvious answers.

I nod and giggle again.

"Damn, who are you tonight?" she asks.

"I'm a mermaid," I say, "Or a sea nymph."

"Yes, you are!" shouts Jasmine.

I'm noticing things I haven't noticed before. Like how every grain of sand under my feet feels like a tiny hand massaging my soles. A single piece of hair blows ever so gently on the side of Emberly's head. At first, I think I'd like to be that hair, but then I decide that being hair would be weird and I'd rather be a tiny version of myself living on the piece of hair.

"Delta," Emberly says with an intensity that makes me think it's not the first time she's said my name.

I shake my head, and the stars in the sky behind her head go all streaky. "Huh?" I ask because I'm not sure if Emberly said something after she said my name.

Jasmine lets out a big laugh. "You're really starting to feel it now, aren't you?"

"Hmmm," I say. "I guess I am." A fit of giggles overtakes me.

Emberly squeezes my hand. "Let's take a walk." She pulls me toward the water and away from the fire.

I'm lagging behind, the sand being extra slippery under my feet. My head's kind of spinning, the stars doing that streaky thing.

"Can we sit?" It comes out kind of breathy, hopefully more sexy than winded.

Emberly guides me to the ground, like I'm a toddler needing help off the swings. I rest my head on her shoulder and squeeze my eyes shut, but I can still feel the world spinning.

"What's going on with you?" Emberly asks, her mouth pressed against the top of my head.

I'm overcome with the urge to put my mouth on her skin. I tilt my head until I can press my lips against her neck. I dart my tongue out and taste so much more than a hint of chlorine. She's heat and spice and I can't get enough of her.

My tongue trails its way down her neck to her clavicle. I reach under her shirt to touch the skin of her stomach. She moans softly, and I want to make her do that a million times over.

My hands slide up a little farther when she gasps. "Delta, wait."

I freeze, then add a breadth of space between my lips and her neck, pause my hands just off her chest.

"Too much?" I ask, my breath whispering over her skin.

"Any other night, no." Even without touching her, I can feel her chest moving up and down. "Tonight, though, with the smoking, and you've been drinking, too, haven't you?"

I nod, my voice stuck in my throat with the direction this conversation has taken.

"This isn't like you." She fidgets with her bracelet, working it around her wrist over and over again.

I flop down on my back in the sand. She lies down next to me. I turn my head away, ashamed to look her in the face as hot tears sting my eyes. Now the stars streak for a different reason.

This summer, I cried in front of her more times than I care to remember, but those were all for a different reason than tonight. A worthier reason.

"Delta, look at me." Emberly reaches around and gently touches my chin. "Please."

I do as she asks. Because even though I'm not sure who I am anymore, I do know one thing. I'm in love with Emberly.

My tears burn as they slip sideways down my face into the sand, almost like the salt of them is scraping my skin.

"I want to do so many things with you," Emberly says. "But those things can wait until we're both sober. That way we make sure neither of us regrets anything."

I nod because I can't speak past the lump in my

throat. She holds me as I cry into her shoulder for the millionth-and-one time. Because earlier I almost did a really stupid thing and one of the worst people in the world stopped me from doing it. And also because Gemma will never get to know this beautiful person I love.

Loving Emberly is the most wonderful thing to ever happen to me. And it's all happening at the worst time of my life.

Chapter 14

My phone alarm rings the next morning, and I wake to a pounding headache and cotton in my mouth. I have no recollection of how I got home or into my bed. My feet are sandy and my hair and clothes are crunchy.

It takes a few tries for me to find the right swipe to turn off the repeating melody on my phone.

There are a ton of unread messages on my phone. The earliest ones are from Jasmine about the upcoming party at the Sea Glass Lodge. Then they turn to Jasmine asking where I am, followed by Emberly wondering the same thing. The last one is in all caps with Jasmine swearing at me that I better be okay. They must have found me at the beach after that.

Last night's events come rushing back to me as a wave of nausea hits. I run to the bathroom but don't get sick, though I think I might feel better if I actually puked. I can't believe I got so drunk and stoned that when I hit on Emberly, she promptly rejected me.

I peel off last night's clothes and take a shower that doesn't feel nearly long enough. I know I can't linger too long or I'll make Emberly late for school. That is if she still plans on picking me up. I hope I didn't do anything worse than what I remember. Thankfully, I don't have to worry long before a beep sounds outside and I find Emberly's car idling outside.

I'm a hungover cliche in sunglasses when I get in the passenger seat, a grateful one because I still seem to have a girlfriend this morning.

"You okay?" Emberly asks.

"I've been better." It's the first time we've been in the car together since our heated kiss from yesterday morning. At least it's the first time I remember being in the car since then because I realize Emberly is probably the one who gave me a ride home last night.

"Should I be thanking you for putting me to bed last night?" My stomach lurches as Emberly pulls away from the curb.

"Yup." A smile plays at her lips, so I know she's not mad. "How bad was waking up?"

"It wasn't my favorite moment," I admit. "But seriously, thank you. I didn't realize smoking weed would mess me up so badly."

"How much of last night do you remember?" There's an edge to her voice.

My face warms, and I stare out the passenger window. "Enough." Once again, I hope nothing more embarrassing happened than having my girlfriend turn me down from making it past second base because I was too wasted.

She was right to do it. Not that I would have regretted doing anything with her, but I'd rather be totally with it for all of those moments with Emberly.

I can feel her studying me in stolen glances while driving, and I awkwardly try and fill the silence.

"So my parents are gone until next week." As soon as I say it, I realize it sounds like I'm trying to seduce her or something. I was going to invite her over, but I know I've made it weird.

"You want me to come over after practice?" Emberly asks, and manages to save me from myself...as always.

"Yeah, if you want." My attempt to be nonchalant

comes out dismissive. I'm screwing up more than normal this morning.

Emberly pulls into a spot in the student parking lot, then looks at me with a smile. "Of course I want to."

"I'll order pizza." My sister was always super hungry after swim practice, so I figure having food is a good thing.

Emberly reaches for my hand as we head toward the school building. I could get used to this new routine of ours.

The others from last night are hanging out by the door. Jasmine is chatting with Camille, who is holding Logan's hand. My stomach gives another lurch, and I swallow down sourness.

When Jasmine sees me, she smiles big and raises her eyebrows. "Party girl!"

Parker laughs, and Briggs whistles provocatively.

"Ugh," I actually say out loud, and Emberly squeezes my hand.

"You ready for more partying Saturday night?" Jasmine asks.

Aside from Logan pulling me out of the water and the fact that I made a fool of myself with Emberly, last night was manageable. In the sense that I was around people other than Jasmine and Emberly and I didn't have a panic attack. That's progress.

"I might be persuaded," I tell Jasmine.

She ditches the others and walks into school with me and Emberly.

"What were you and Camille talking about?" I ask.

"Just swim stuff." Jasmine's trying to act nonchalant, but she's very pointedly not looking at me. It's shady that she was talking to Camille...almost like they were conspiring.

"Don't you think it's time we maybe forgave her?"

Jasmine asks.

The tension in the hallway is thick, and I know Emberly can feel it based on the way her hand twitches in mine.

"Are you suggesting that we forgive the traitor who hooked up with Gemma's boyfriend before her body was even cold?"

We stop in front of Jasmine's homeroom, clogging up the doorway. Three days into school and I've already made a scene in this hallway twice. But what Jasmine is suggesting is worth making a stink over. The whole damn thing stinks worse than my sister's rotten ghost smell.

"You seemed to have forgiven Logan based on the way you two were sharing that joint last night," Jasmine says loudly, the crowd around us growing larger by the minute.

"Just because I smoked his weed, doesn't mean I forgive him." Logan and I may have had a moment in the water, but that's not an act of me forgiving him for being with Camille.

Jasmine's arms are folded across her chest and her eyes are narrowed. It hurts that she's the one betraying me now. The ever-present storm surges inside me, hovering too close to the surface, threatening to burst out of me in a tsunami of destruction. I attempt a deep breath, but it fails to temper the storm.

"They're happy together." Every word Jasmine speaks feeds the storm. "Not everyone has to be miserable like you, Delta. You've been moping around all summer. You don't have to keep hating on them just so you have someone other than yourself to hate on."

I bite my bottom lip and ball my fists at my side to keep the storm from raging out of control. In our twelve years of friendship, we've had plenty of fights—shouting matches and physical altercations alike—but I have never in my life been so mad at her as I am right now.

Emberly's gaze darts between me and Jasmine. I'm not sure when it happened, but I'm no longer holding her hand. Instead, I'm right in front of Jasmine, her back against the corner of the door frame.

Not that Jasmine is cowering under my wrath. No, her brown eyes spark fire at me.

"Maybe this isn't the best time to talk about this," Emberly says.

"Stay out of it, Emberly." Jasmine shoots a deadly look in her direction. "It's none of your business. You don't know what it was like before. How close we were with Camille."

"Don't talk to her like that." My voice is a gale-force wind, gusty and powerful.

Jasmine's fire turns back on me. "Gemma's dead, Delta. And that sucks...for all of us. But with you blaming all your bad feelings on Camille, it's like I've lost her too. And I don't want to lose any more friends."

"Fine," I say and I try to put as much poison into my next words as I can. "You don't have to lose Camille. But if you want to be friends with her, then you're fucking losing me as a best friend."

Chapter 15

I push my way through all the gawkers as the early warning bell rings and sprint to the back stairwell. Hardly anyone uses it, so I head down half a flight of stairs to an empty landing.

My whole body is warm and buzzing. Last week this surely would have stolen my breath and sent me into a panic attack, but I'm too full of anger to fall victim to that. My storm is keeping me full of air. I'm a dangerous gust of wind, ready to spin into a hurricane.

The list of betrayals grows long. I can't believe Jasmine would side with Camille. I'm Gemma's sister, and Jasmine's judging me for the way I'm grieving her. She should be judging Camille, but she wants to forgive that traitor.

Every new hurt is a stark reminder of the agony I felt when my mom told me Gemma was dead. I can't separate any of my feelings from it; they all get tied up in Gemma's death. They swirl together, and now I'm a storm on the brink of being out of control. I'm on a path where everything succumbs to the storm.

I don't expect Jasmine to feel the same way I do, but she could at least try to understand that this isn't something I can just move on from. I'm not trying to be moody and sad all the time. I want to be happy, but any happiness I achieve is fleeting and tainted with guilt. How can I be happy when my sister is dead?

And then I'm left with the all-consuming emptiness that Gemma left behind that I'll never be able to fill.

The betrayal of Jasmine not understanding this, or rather her not trying to understand because no one can truly comprehend how I feel about losing Gemma, may be worse than Camille's...if it's true that Camille and Logan are simply trying to find happiness in each other. I'm not saying I necessarily believe Logan, but there was a ring of truth to what he told me.

But every time I try to find an ounce of forgiveness for Camille, Gemma's ghost fills my mind. Her desperate pleas and silent screams. Something terrible is going on with her soul, or whatever she is. Or my mind is playing tricks on me.

It hasn't escaped me that it's possible that Gemma's ghost is all in my head. That she is less apparition, more hallucination. A way for my mind to try and make sense of her death. Not that her death will ever make sense.

Yet, she seemed so real, right down to the fetid scent of rot. How could all that be a figment of my imagination?

I huddle in the corner of the landing, my legs tucked up to my chest, my arms wrapped tight around them. I'm so tired of being in my own head. The more the thoughts spiral, the more I don't blame Jasmine for wanting to be friends with Camille instead of me. Jasmine's right, I'm mopey and boring.

The door above opens with a bang. "Delta?" Emberly's hesitant call echoes down to me.

"I'm here," I say into my knees.

Emberly's footsteps proceed down the stairs. She sits down next to me, her smooth leg pressed against the arm that firmly clutches my bent knees.

"I told Mrs. Chamberlain that you were here but you needed a few minutes. You okay?"

"Did the whole school hear that?" I keep my face

pressed into my knees to avoid what must be a look of pity on Emberly's face.

"Well..." she sighs. "I mean, yeah, a lot of people did."

She shifts and the spot on my arm where her leg no longer makes contact quickly grows cold. Then she rubs her hand across my skin in a soothing way and the warmth returns. "Do you want me to take you home?"

I chance a glance at her. There's worry in her eyes but not pity.

A part of me needs to know why she's here, even if I'll regret asking when I find out. "How can you stand to stay with me? It's like Jasmine said, I'm a miserable human being."

"You're not miserable," Emberly insists in her quiet way. "You're sad and mourning a terrible loss. Jasmine is, too, and you both don't know where to put all that grief because you can't put it on each other, or anyone else who loved your sister."

"But that doesn't make it okay for me to put it on you, just because you didn't know Gemma." I'm back to hiding my face.

"And you don't. Talking about how you're feeling isn't putting these feelings on me." Emberly rests the side of her head on my shoulder, her hair tickling the skin on my arms. The points of contact with her keep me grounded, out of my head.

"But I'm not any fun to be around," I protest.

"I had fun with you this summer."

"You did?" I peek at her again, and she's looking right at me, smiling.

"I did."

"Even though we didn't do much and I was mopey and sad."

"I don't think you acted as sad as you think you did." She nudges me with her knee in a playful way. "Besides, if anyone had a reason to be sad, it's you."

"So I *was* sad all the time." I blow out a frustrated breath. I wish I could blow this storm right out of me, but it refuses to be dislodged.

"I already said you weren't." She nudges me again, and I know she's trying to cheer me up. "Just because our summer was low-key doesn't mean it was sad or boring. You helped me get to know a new place, full of new people, at my pace."

That makes me smile. "I did?"

"Yeah." She nods emphatically. "It was just what I needed. And even if I thought you were sad and boring—which I don't—it's okay to feel your feelings."

"Thanks for giving me the space to do that." The closeness of our bodies grounds me, quells the storm...for now. "You still wanna come over tonight?"

"Of course."

I straighten up and stretch my legs. I pull her in for a kiss and our lips stay together. I close my eyes and deepen the kiss, and Emberly responds with all the enthusiasm I could hope for.

When we pull away from each other, Emberly hands me a slip of paper. "I got you a pass for being late to first period."

"You're the best."

We hold each other another minute, and I try to be present to enjoy this moment of happiness, whether it's tainted with guilt or not. I'm still mad at Jasmine, but she's right that I can't spend the rest of my life being miserable and boring.

Chapter 16

Thoughts of being alone with Emberly tonight help me power through another day of school. Logan tries to make eye contact when I get into AP history, but I ignore him. My emotions are too raw to deal with him, though I feel my resolve to hate him softening. I want to hate him but can't find the heart for it.

I find I'm actually able to concentrate in class and it goes by faster than it ever has before. When I get off the bus and unlock the door to my house, a murmuring from upstairs nearly has me walking right back out. But I'm not letting anything, not even noisy intruders, ruin my night with Emberly.

I creep up the stairs, a man's voice getting louder as I go. At the top, where you can either go right to mine and Gemma's room or left into my parents' room, I can tell the voice is coming from the left. I catch the word "savings" and "insurance."

"It's the freakin' radio," I mutter to myself.

Sure enough, my stepdad's radio is blaring in my parents' room. He must have forgotten to turn off his alarm, and that means the radio has been on all day.

I'm about to turn it off when the commercial ends and the weather report catches my attention.

"The big story we're tracking is the path of Hurricane Ophelia," a man says in a deep newscaster voice. "Currently the category one hurricane has stalled out in the Atlantic well off the coast of eastern Florida. It continues to strengthen and is expected to become a category two hurricane overnight."

Earlier, I almost had myself convinced that Gemma's ghost was a figment of my imagination, but her warning about a storm comes ringing back to me.

"The National Weather Service is tracking this storm closely with some models showing it could potentially impact the southern and mid-Atlantic states Friday evening into Saturday, and have significant impacts on New York City and the northeast Saturday night into Sunday."

My heart goes into a panic as my brain makes the connection between the party scheduled for Saturday night and when the storm is predicted to hit.

Beware the storm.

The radio guy continues to blather on and I frantically search for the off button, my heart rate going up with each word. "Now we go live to meteorologists Kate Jenson, who is standing by in Cape Hatteras, North Carolina, as residents brace for the storm."

I yank the radio plug from the outlet before I have to listen to anything Kate Jenson has to say about the hurricane. My brain fights over the conflicting thoughts of "beware the storm" and "Gemma's ghost is only in my imagination."

I head to my room where I try to concentrate on the assignments I've let pile up since the start of school. My phone rings, offering a real distraction. I'm praying it's not Emberly calling to cancel when I see that it's my mom.

"Hi, Mom," I say.

"Delta!" she shouts, even though it's a phone and there's no need to yell. "Have you heard about the hurricane? Gary says it's headed straight for Connecticut."

"I heard about it." Seems everything is about a storm

lately.

"Gary's keeping a close eye on its path. If it stays on this course, I want you to take a bus up to Grandma's. I don't want you home alone during a hurricane."

"Stop worrying, Mom. It'll probably go out to sea." There was no mention of that on the forecast, but hurricanes change paths all the time. It's been years since we've had one impact us, so there's no need to "beware the storm."

"Promise me you'll catch a bus if it looks like it's going to be bad," my mom says.

"How about I go to Jasmine's house?" Not that I'd do that after this morning's very public fight, but my mom doesn't have to know about that. I can always stay with Emberly...probably, if it's okay with her parents.

"Fine," my mom agrees. Her voice gets a little muffled, but I can still hear her as she talks to my stepdad. "Maybe we catch a flight home today."

"Mom!" I yell into the phone. "Don't come home and ruin your vacation. Mom!"

"Okay, okay," she says in a muted voice before talking to me again. "Your stepfather agrees that there's no need to come home. As long as you go to Jasmine's this weekend."

"Yes, I'll go to Jasmine's." Definitely not. Maybe Emberly can stay with me all weekend. That would be amazing. "Are you having fun?" I think to ask.

"We are. The beaches here are amazing. And the rum." My mom giggles in a very schoolgirl way. I haven't heard her laugh like that in a long time. My parents need this break, and I'm not going to ruin it for them.

"Go have more fun...and rum," I say. "Love you, Mom."

"Love you too, sweetheart. Be safe."

I click off the call and stare at my laptop, the cursor blinking on a blank page where I'm supposed to be working on my AP history assignment. That's not happening right now.

Besides, I have to prepare for Emberly's visit. I have no idea if we'll end up in my bed this evening or not, but just in case we do, I brush all the sand from last night off my blankets. There's no time to wash anything, so that'll have to be good enough.

I clean some dirty clothes off the floor and make sure there's a fresh hand towel in the bathroom. Growing up sharing a room with my sister and having parents that never went away for more than a night or two here and there, neither Gemma nor I had many opportunities for a significant other to sleep over. The one time my parents went away for New Year's and Logan stayed over, Jasmine and I stayed up late and crashed in the living room. We let Gemma and Logan have full use of the bedroom. That was the first night they had sex.

Gemma was so happy after. She said it was the perfect night and looked all starry-eyed for days after.

And now Logan's with Camille. I don't know for sure that they've had sex, but I'm assuming they have based on all the PDA. That is definitely not what I want to be thinking about tonight. My stomach is queasy enough with nerves, I don't need disgust over Logan and Camille added to that. Tonight is supposed to be about me and Emberly.

Chapter 17

I push away thoughts of the traitors and check the time on my phone. There's still about a half hour before Emberly should be here, and I'm buzzing with nervous energy. I decide to shower because I know Emberly will be freshly showered after swim practice.

Then I take my time picking out an outfit that looks casual enough to say I'm not trying too hard but also nice. I consider borrowing one of Gemma's flowy tank tops—none of us have had the heart to get rid of any of her clothes—the kind of shirt she would never let me borrow when she was alive because I would "mess it all up." I settle for a light blue v-neck and white shorts...and my cutest matching bra and underwear set, just in case.

When I'm done getting ready, I order pizza because I know it will be at least 45 minutes before it'll get delivered. I play on my phone to kill time, careful to avoid any photos or videos of me and Jasmine that are making the rounds.

By the time Emberly's car pulls up in front of my house, I'm hyper-aware of everything about my body and in danger of needing to put on more deodorant. I take a few deep breaths—this is no time for a panic attack—before greeting her at the door.

"Hey," I say.

She leans in for what I think is going to be a kiss that turns into an awkward hug because I'm positioned all wrong for it. Her hair smells like tropical flowers without even a hint of chlorine.

"I washed my hair twice," she says as if she knows I'm

smelling it.

I run my hand down the back of her head, neck, and back, all the way to where the waves of her hair end. "It looks nice."

I'm now self-conscious about the messy bun I threw my hair into after my shower. I should have put as much thought into my hair as I did into my outfit. Emberly looks adorable in sweatshorts in the school colors of red and navy blue and an off-the-shoulder white t-shirt that says, "Sleep, eat, swim. Repeat." In the living room, Emberly sets her bag down on the chair my stepdad usually sits in.

"The pizza should be here soon. You wanna just hang out here until then?" I ask.

"Sure."

We're being more awkward than usual, the possibility of what might happen this evening affecting our normal, easy way with each other. We sit on the couch together, close but not touching. Emberly plays with her bracelet, while I turn on the TV and click on the icon of a long-running drama series Gemma and I watched a million times.

"Oh, I love this one," Emberly says. "I mean it's kind of stupid with the love triangle turned rectangle or whatever you call it."

"A love rectangle! That's what Gemma used to call it." I always made fun of her for it, but it's cute when Emberly says it.

Pretty soon we're laughing at the romantic parts and cheering during the fight scenes. We've inched closer and closer until my arm is on the back of the couch behind Emberly and her leg is slung over my thigh.

When the pizza gets here, I put the show on my tablet and we watch another episode while standing at the kitchen counter eating pizza. Emberly laughs particularly hard at the scene where the half-werewolf partly transforms as the ghost-hunting girl kisses him. I pop a pepperoni into her mouth and that makes her laugh even harder.

When she's done chewing, she licks a spot of pizza sauce off her finger. A sort of popping noise goes off in my head as I stare at her. When she notices me looking, the mood in the room changes.

She waves her greasy fingers. "Do you mind if I clean up in your bathroom?"

"Sure," I say. "It's straight up the stairs."

"I remember."

Emberly's been here a few times, but we prefer her house, and its access to the private beach. Honestly, the whole place has been depressing with my parents sad and exhausted all the time, and boring me the only other person here.

I twist my thoughts away from that and back to Emberly. I follow her into the living room where the stairs are.

She's halfway up when I ask, "You want me to bring your bag up? We can watch the rest of the show in my room."

"Sure. I'll meet you there."

I rush back to the kitchen and put the dirty dishes in the dishwasher. Then I grab my tablet and Emberly's bag and head upstairs.

She's sitting on the edge of my bed when I get there, but she springs up when she sees me.

"Hey!" she says.

"Hey. You can sit."

I smile to try and put her at ease as she sits back

down, but I'm as keyed up as she seems to be. I decide to be brave and put it all out there about how I'm feeling.

"I'm really glad you're staying over tonight." Not terribly insightful but the truth.

"Me too. I told my mom a bunch of us from the swim team are staying at Jasmine's tonight. I hope that's okay."

I don't want to talk about Jasmine, but it's not Emberly's fault her swim teammates make for a good excuse to stay at her girlfriend's house on a school night.

"Yeah, it's fine." I drop her bag next to my bed, take a seat at my desk chair, and put the tablet down, not quite ready to be with Emberly on my bed, not until I let her know what I expect out of tonight.

We both start talking at the same time, me with "look" and her with "I just."

"You go," she says.

"I was going to say that just because you're staying here tonight doesn't mean we have to do anything in particular. I'm not...I haven't..." I take a deep breath and plunge right in. "What I'm trying to say is that I want to do things with you, but only things that you—we're both— ready to do."

Emberly smiles her sweetest smile. "That's pretty much what I was gonna say." She pats the bed. "Do you want to turn the show back on and join me?"

"I do." I flip open the tablet case and turn the show to where we left off downstairs.

I scoot back on the bed until my back is against the side wall. Then I reach for Emberly's hand and she scoots back next to me.

We hold hands and Emberly rests her head on my shoulder. By the end of the episode, I notice her head has gotten very heavy and her breathing has grown slow and steady. She's sound asleep. It must've been a demanding swim practice.

It's grown dark outside my window. Inside my room, the glow of the screen is the only light. The next episode starts and I try to stay as still as possible, so as not to wake her. It's not the night I imagined, but Emberly has supported me so much these last two months, the least I can do is be a shoulder for her to sleep on.

Chapter 18

I'm on my side, facing Gemma's bed. She's there, but something feels wrong about it. It take me a minute to realize what that is.

"You're supposed to be dead," I say.

"I am." It sounds like her real voice, not that ghostly one.

"You're dead or you're supposed to be dead?"

She folds her arms across her chest. "What does that even mean, Delta?"

It's such a Gemma thing to say. I jump up to hug her, and she's flesh and bone.

"Oh, god," I say. "It's really you, not that weird ghost you."

"Ghost me?" She tilts her head like she can't make sense of me, but she's the one who's supposed to be dead. "What are you talking about?"

"Never mind that." There are more important things to talk about. "Are you okay? I mean, you're dead so you're not okay. Are you okay for a dead person?"

"I'm not following." She's staring at me like I've gone mad, and well, she's probably on to something there.

"Your ghost has been haunting me, and it was in pain or tortured or something."

"I'm not a ghost, Delta." She pinches my arm, and I yelp with the sharp zing of pain.

"That's for dreams," I remind her. "And you're supposed to do it to yourself, not me." She pinches me again.

This back-and-forth between us, it's just like old times. This is the stuff I miss the most. Me being annoying and her pretending like she has no idea what I'm talking about.

"Gemma, how are you here?" I don't know why I'm questioning the logic of what's happening when I should be enjoying hanging out with my sister. It's only now that she's here that I realize that this is what I've wanted all these months, a chance to hang out with her.

"It's your dream, silly," Gemma says. "I don't know how it works."

"My dream?"

That doesn't make sense. She pinched me and I felt it, so how is this a dream? Confusing me even more is that when I look back at her on the bed, it's ghost Gemma that sits there, not the real Gemma from a minute ago. In the place where her heart should be, glows the red heart-shaped piece of sea glass.

"No," I say. "Where's the real Gemma? You're not the real Gemma. You're an impostor."

Her mouth opens in that silent scream, only it's not silent this time. The scream is so loud and high, it feels like my head is going to explode. I clamp my hands over my ears, but it doesn't help. It's like the scream is coming from inside my head. Pieces of sea glass rain down on us. The edges have the frosty blunt look of weathered sea glass, but when they hit my skin, they're as sharp as fresh shards. Tiny cuts blossom red all over my arms.

Gemma's ghostly voice screams, "Beware the storm. Beware the storm. Beware the storm."

I awake to my own scream, and someone shouts in surprise next to me. I scramble away to the top of my bed.

"Delta?" Emberly says in a sleepy voice.

"Oh shit," I say. "Emberly, it's just you."

The tablet has gone dark. A slant of light from the street lamp shines in the window. The jar of sea glass sits harmlessly on Gemma's nightstand, the red piece indistinguishable from the others in the dark.

"Bad dream?" Emberly asks. She reaches over and gently rubs my arms, which are peppered with goose bumps instead of tiny cuts.

"It wasn't." I think of the banter between me and Gemma in my dream, how good that felt. But it all went wrong when she turned into ghost Gemma. "Then it was bad."

She slides right next to me and places a hand on my chest. "Your heart's beating really fast. You okay?"

"It's not a panic attack." She's been around for enough of those to know the signs, but that's not what this is. "It was just the dream."

She rests her head on my chest. "I fell asleep on you, didn't I?"

She's changing the subject, and I love her for that.

"You did." I kiss the top of her head. "But then I fell asleep, too."

She yawns, her jaw rubbing against where her face is pressed against my chest. "It was a hard practice. We're working on our exchanges for the relay. I'm awake now, though, I promise."

"You sure?" I tease.

She looks up at me with her big brown eyes. "Oh, I'm sure." Then she gently kisses the skin just above the v of my shirt.

I tuck all thoughts of that awful dream away and let other, much more pleasant ones fill my head.

Emberly slowly kisses her way up my neck to my

mouth. Our lips meet and it sets my body on fire. The kiss quickly turns greedy, like neither one of us can get enough of the other. Her body is pressed against mine almost as hard as our lips are pressed together. I reach for her hip and slide one finger under her shirt.

I don't want to stop kissing her, but I want to make sure she's ready before I go any further. "Is this okay?"

"Yes." She puts her hand on mine and guides it all the way under her shirt and up the smooth skin of her strong swimmer's back.

We press our lips back together, while our hands explore new places. This time no one is drunk or high. This time there is no hesitation or worries about regrets. We're all in, and I lose myself in this person I'm falling in love with.

Chapter 19

Confusion washes over me when I wake up tangled up in a sheet and someone else's legs. Then I smell Emberly's tropical shampoo and lay perfectly still so as not to wake her. Everything about last night washes over me, and I grin into Emberly's hair, her head tucked on my chest.

We didn't fall right back to sleep after we were done kissing and touching and exploring. We agreed it might not be comfortable to actually sleep while naked, so we giggled in the dark while we searched for our pajamas. Neither one of us suggested turning on a light, though it would have been easier to get dressed. I think we were both afraid it would disrupt the magic of our first night together. There was something about being cloaked in darkness that made the whole thing feel like it never had to end.

But now it's morning and light is streaming in because we never bothered to shut the blinds. Even in the daylight, I feel the magic of this girl in bed with me.

I'm happy in a way that I haven't been in a long time. This giddiness has pierced through my grief in a way nothing else has. It's not gone, but it's not taking up all the space anymore. I don't think I'll ever stop missing my sister, but right now it doesn't feel like my world begins and ends with that grief. There is room for something else in there, too.

"I love you," I whisper into Emberly's hair.

She stirs and reaches for my hand without taking her head off my chest. Our hands entwine.

"Did you say something?" she asks before yawning.

I almost say no, but I'm feeling bold enough this morning to say it so I know she'll hear it. "I love you."

That gets her to raise her head. Her grin is the biggest I've ever seen it. "I love you, too."

"You do?"

In answer, she caresses my cheek with her thumb. "I do."

Then we're kissing and it's so good that I never want to stop. But it's a school day, so before we get carried away, we force ourselves out of bed and get ready. The day is sunny and bright, and even if it were pouring rain, I don't think it would dampen my mood.

We grab bananas and make it to the car with time to spare. Emberly doesn't start it up right away but stares straight ahead out the windshield, her forehead scrunched up in thought. A worried, tangled sensation rolls through my stomach. I wrack my brain trying to think of something I did wrong last night, but everything except for that stupid dream felt perfect.

She bites her bottom lip in a way that makes me want to head right back to my room. Then she turns her solemn expression on me. "I heard something yesterday that worried me."

So whatever is bothering her has nothing to do with last night. It would be a relief but for the fact that she's clearly upset.

"You can tell me," I assure her.

"I know," she says. "It's just I don't want to upset you. Last night was amazing and you seem in such a good place this morning."

"I am," I say slowly, trying to figure out where this conversation is going. Emberly's worried about something that she thinks might upset me, but I have no idea what that is. Does she think I'm a porcelain doll that will crack at any moment? I suppose if she does, it's my fault for the way I've been acting all summer. It's actually taken a great deal of strength to hold back the storm of grief.

"Talk to me, Emberly."

"Okay," she says matter-of-factly as she turns back to look out the windshield. "So you know how I told everyone that I was out of swimming for a while because I hurt my shoulder and had to rehab it?"

"Yeah," I say. "And it was shortly after your shoulder healed up that you moved here and started swimming again."

"My parents made me tell that story," she says quickly, like she's ripping off the band-aid of a lie.

"A story?" I say. "So it's not true."

"It wasn't a shoulder injury that kept me from swimming." Tears shine in her eyes, and she refuses to look at me. I want to wrap her up in a hug and tell her that whatever it is, I'm okay with it, but it seems like she needs space right now.

"Do you want to tell me what it was?"

"I do," she hesitates. "It's just I'm afraid of how it will make you feel. You've been so sad since we met and I don't want to push you to..."

I stare at Emberly quizzically, but she refuses to look at me. Maybe if she did, it would help me put the pieces together of what she's trying to tell me. I don't understand what her thing with swimming has to do with me, except for her coming clean about lying. But it feels like more than that.

I knew the magic of our night wouldn't last forever, but I hoped it would at least make it until we got to school.

Chapter 20

Afraid I'm going to regret finding out what's bothering Emberly, I say, "I don't understand."

She's twisting her bracelet around her wrist hard enough that it must be chaffing her skin, but she doesn't seem to notice. "What happened the other night at the beach before I showed up?"

She's giving me whiplash with the change in topic. "I drank and smoked with Logan, Parker, and Briggs. I know it was stupid. I was just letting off some steam."

Emberly goes still and looks at me, desperation in her eyes. "And that's all that happened?"

Is she afraid I cheated on her? Did she freak out on a cheating ex and get suspended from the swim team and that's why her parents moved her here?

"You don't think...Emberly, I would never cheat on you."

"It's not that." She takes a deep breath, her chest heaving up and then going back down. "What did you go down to that beach to do? Without your phone, without letting anyone know where you were going?"

My pulse hitches up and my breathing becomes shallow. "I told you, I went for a walk and forgot my phone. Then I ran into Logan and the others and joined them."

"And the wading in the water, when did you do that?" She's back to playing with her bracelet.

Why is she grilling me like this? If it's not smoking or cheating that's got her upset, then what is it? She has no way of knowing the other thing I did that night that could upset her. Unless Logan told her how he found me in the water.

It takes everything I have in me not to bolt out of the car. "What did Logan tell you?"

The tears spill over Emberly's lashes onto her cheeks. "Camille said—"

"Camille?" I'm shouting now. "Why would you be talking to her? And about me!"

"Logan told her he found you in the water. That you were just lying there, like you were waiting for it to wash up over and...and..." Emberly lets out a sob.

I'm too angry for her tears to affect me. "So you and Camille had a nice little chat about me. Poor depressed Delta, who can't get over her dead sister. Poor suicidal Delta!"

"Are you?" Emberly reaches for me, but I slide away in my seat until I'm right up against the passenger door. "Have you been thinking about taking your own life?"

"Fuck, Emberly!" My hand is on the door handle, ready to get the hell out of here. "That's what this conversation is about. You think I'm...you think."

I don't know why I'm so angry, it seems she's only concerned for me, and with good reason because I was on a dangerous edge that night on the beach. The storm was calm in me, and I was ready to let go.

If only it hadn't been Camille that told her about it. It makes my skin crawl to think of the two of them talking about me, pitying me. Jasmine was probably in on it too; it's the kind of gossip she craves.

I have the door half open when Emberly grabs my arm more aggressively than she's ever touched me. She clutches me so hard, her nails dig into my skin.

"Wait, Delta," she says, the tears really flowing down

her pink cheeks.

"No." I put one leg out the door. "I don't need to hear what you and Camille think about poor Delta."

She won't let go of my arm. Her nails dig in so hard, she draws blood.

"Let go of me," I say with as much poison as I can put into my voice. She's ruining last night; she's ruining everything.

"No, you can't go."

"I'm going." It stings when I yank my arm away and leave behind a chunk of skin.

I'm out of the car and about to slam the door when Emberly screams, "I tried to kill myself!"

That stops me in my tracks, and a chill runs down my spine. I duck my head back into the open car door. "What?"

"That's why I had to take a break from swimming. I took a bunch of my mom's pills one night and fell out of my bed. My parents came to check on me and couldn't wake me." Her words come quickly until she stops to take a breath that sounds more like a sob.

I get back in the car and shut the door as quietly as I can.

She takes a minute to breathe through it, but there are still tears running down her cheeks when she continues. "They took me to the hospital, and after I had to go to an in-patient place for a few weeks. Then they moved us here. We couldn't go too far because of my dad's job, but they didn't want to stay where we were."

"Shit, Emberly. I had no idea." I feel awful for freaking out on her, even if she's been talking to Camille.

"How could you know? I didn't tell anyone. Not even my swim friends. They really do think I had a shoulder injury." She's stopped crying at least.

There's blood seeping from the wound on my arm and I rub it away with an angry swipe. I'm still angry, but I'm not going to run away. I won't do that to Emberly, who has been here for me through all of my shit.

"So why tell me now?" I ask, though I don't think I'm going to like the answer.

"Because if that's how you're feeling now or if that's how you've been feeling, I want you to know that I've felt it too. And I'm here for you." She shakily reaches for my hand and I let her take it, feel the tremble of her fingers in mine. "Jasmine and Camille are here for you, too...if you'd let them."

"Don't." I pull my hand from hers. "I can't with them right now." The thought of the three of them talking about me behind my back churns the storm in my gut, but I think it's a storm of anger, not grief.

"Okay," she agrees. "Please let me do one thing, though. Can I put a number in your phone that you can call if you ever feel that way?"

I hand over my phone. Her hands shake as she types in a number she gets from her phone. I can tell it will make her feel better if I let her do this, not that I'll ever call it. What would I say? *My dead sister is haunting me. She's warning me 'beware the storm.' But some days I want the storm to come and sweep up every shit moment of my life without her.*

She hands back the phone. "Thanks for letting me do that."

My lip twitches in the approximation of a repentant half-smile. Emberly's courage in telling me what happened to her has dissipated some of my anger. Still, it's going to take some time to get over the sting of her talking to Camille about me.

"Thanks for telling me the truth." I smile for real and try to bring my mind back to the magic of last night when there weren't all these bad feelings bouncing between us.

My phone pings with a message from my mom, but the time on the display distracts me from reading it. "We're going to be late for school."

"That's okay, we can get a note," Emberly says. "One thing I learned in my time recovering, is that school, swimming, even family can wait. You've got to make sure you're okay first."

I hear what she's saying, and I can appreciate she thinks she can relate to what's going on with me, but no one really knows what Gemma's death has done to me.

The wind in my lungs trying to tear me apart from the inside.

The pouring rain in my heart drowning out my feelings.

The churning waves pounding away at my stomach.

My budding love for Emberly broke through for a minute there, but it seems nothing is stronger than grief.

Chapter 21

When I get to homeroom, I'm antsy from raw emotions. Emberly's bombshell can only go so far to soften the blow of talking about me behind my back. And with Camille of all people. My brain reasons that her actions come from a place of concern, but my heart stings with yet another betrayal.

It's no wonder I nearly fall out of my seat when everyone's phones start blaring an emergency alert. Once the homeroom teacher realizes it's about the hurricane, she lets everyone stop hiding their phones under the table. She reads the alert aloud and I read along silently as if these are the instructions for the SATs.

A hurricane warning and a bunch of other warnings have been issued for Connecticut's entire coastline. The worst impacts are predicted for Saturday evening into Sunday morning. The alert then goes on to list a bunch of recommendations on how to prepare for the storm.

While the teacher is reading through the long list, her lips pinched into a frown and her voice a droning monotone, an announcement breaks over the loudspeaker. The principal, who I've never heard make any kind of announcement, comes on.

"Attention faculty, staff, and students. In light of the weather warnings at the approach of Hurricane Ophelia, there will be an early dismissal today and all after-school activities for this afternoon and evening have been canceled, as well as any school-related activities for the weekend." She blathers on for another few minutes about safety and dismissal times, but no one's really listening.

The atmosphere in the room has turned electric. Whispered conversations break out all over the room. I overhear much speculation on whether or not the party at the Sea Glass Lodge will be canceled. By now all the upperclassmen and probably some sophomores, too, have heard about it.

The teacher excuses herself to the hallway where several other teachers have gathered.

Now that she's gone, the pretense of keeping quiet is no longer necessary.

Briggs stands up. "Guys, calm down." He glances at the door, but none of the teachers are paying attention to us. "Parker's already had the kegs delivered. Spread the word, we're not gonna let a little storm keep us from partying."

A cheer rings out, and the teacher looks at us with concern through the glass window in the door. It doesn't matter because the bell rings to signal the end of homeroom.

The hallways are more crowded than usual as I navigate my way to first period. People are darting about with a frantic energy, it's louder than normal with high-pitched conversations, and I keep having to dodge around people. It's like a bunch of golden retriever puppies have escaped into the hallway.

My social circle is basically down to one: Emberly. And even that relationship is rocky right now, so I have no one I'm interested in seeking out. Instead of running about looking for people to gossip with about the hurricane, all my anxieties are turned inward.

My magical night with Emberly, and the sour turn it took this morning, pushed the nightmare about Gemma to the back of my mind. News of the storm has brought it back to the forefront.

Beware the storm.

Ever since that first ghostly visit the night before school started, I've been going back and forth about whether it was really her ghost or a figment of my imagination. That dream last night proves she's invaded my subconscious, so maybe all those ghostly visits were from my own mind as well.

If there's one thing Gemma's death has taught me is that grief is different for everyone. That's why when my mom and I are out in public and acquaintances ask how she's been and she goes on and on about how sad she is—to the point where the other person is clearly uncomfortable—I don't say anything to her. That's her brand of grief, and if it makes some random person uncomfortable, oh well. My mom's lost a daughter; we can all extend her extra grace, even at the expense of our own comfort.

Maybe Gemma's ghost is my grief manifesting itself. Just because I don't understand the message, doesn't mean it isn't coming from me. The mind is a strange place.

By the end of first period, I've convinced myself that Gemma's ghost isn't real. It's all in my head, which means I should have control over it. I should be able to make the ghostly visits stop.

Still, I can't shake the uneasy feeling that grips me harder with each passing class. As my classmates, and the teachers too, grow more restless and less attentive, I grow more anxious.

Beware the storm.

Could all of that really have been in my head? Gemma was always the more imaginative of the two of us. When we were kids, she had all these games with tons of characters and adventurous places she made up. I would play, too, but

I was more along for the ride and not the driver of the game. If Gemma said the tree in our backyard was a castle with a fire-breathing dragon guarding the tower and we had to rescue the princess, then I said okay. Not because I could picture the tree as a castle—to me a tree was just a tree—but because Gemma said it was. I'd poke around at the air with my stick to fight the dragon. Gemma saw the stick as a sword and conjured the dragon out of thin air. She was the believer in the power of the imagination, not me.

So who am I to think I could imagine something so detailed and terrifying, right down to the rotten stink of Gemma's ghost? It doesn't track.

Luckily none of our teachers bother to make us do much of anything. My last class of this shortened day is AP biology. Instead of even trying to continue our lesson on the evolution of the peppered moth, our teacher lectures us on hurricane preparedness and sneaks in a few thoughts on climate change.

I wouldn't even know where to start with my house against the storm. I'll go home and look for batteries and a flashlight, but I'm not sure there's much else I can do.

Emberly surprises me at my locker when the school day ends early. "You want a ride home?"

"Sure."

She smiles like it's a regular day, like we didn't have sex last night and she didn't tell me about trying to kill herself. Either she really is okay with everything, or she's really good at pretending. I try to match her normalcy, but like I said, I'm not great at pretending. Her hands swing gently by her sides as we walk out to the parking lot, and it would be so easy to reach out and hold one. Instead, I keep my grip tight on the straps of my backpack.

Emberly's phone chimes with a text, and she groans as she checks it. "It's my mom. She's freaking out about the hurricane. She wants me to stop at the store and get water. Like there'll be any left with everyone already in panic mode."

She smiles at me again, and this time I see the strain in her eyes when I half-heartedly smile back. "Do you want to come to the store with me?"

I shrug. "I've got nothing else to do."

Jasmine, Camille, Logan, and Parker are hanging out by Logan's truck. It's an older Ford with rust marks along the side of the bed, but it worked just fine for getting us all around. Gemma and Camille would always call dibs on the actual seats in the cab, while Jasmine and I, and anyone else who was with us, would sit in the bed. We'd have to lay down the whole ride so we wouldn't get busted by the cops for riding in the back. Thinking about it, I can feel the rush of air on my face and see the treetops, lit up by the streetlights, whipping by as we drove around.

The four of them are yelling to anyone within hearing distance that the party is still on. When they spot me and Emberly, they fall silent. Jasmine pretends to be preoccupied with examining her nails, but Camille shoots me a piercing look that raises the tiny hairs on the back of my neck.

Logan jogs over to meet us at Emberly's car. "You coming to the party?"

"No," I say at the same time as Emberly says, "Maybe."

Logan looks from me to Emberly and back to me. It's clear he doesn't want to get involved in whatever is going on between us, but I know he has something to say based on how his jaw twitches. He would always clench his teeth whenever he and Gemma had a disagreement.

"You should come, Delta," he says, eyeing Emberly. I wonder if they've talked about me behind my back, too. "It'll be better than sitting home and riding out the storm alone."

"Will it?" I shoot back. I see what they're doing, trying to keep an eye on me, so I don't do something stupid. I get in Emberly's car without another word.

"See ya, Logan," Emberly says as she joins me.

She pulls out of the parking lot, and I wait until we've been on the road for a few minutes before asking, "Why did you ask to stay over last night?"

I watch as blush creeps up Emberly's neck. "I wanted to be with you."

"Is that all?" I stare at her intensely, but she keeps her attention on the road.

"Isn't that enough?" She bites her bottom lip and glances at me.

Her lips are distracting me, and I almost quit my line of questioning, but I have to know. "It just feels like everyone thinks I need to be watched, and they nominated you as chief babysitter in charge of Delta."

"Who's 'everyone'?" she asks. "The only person I told where I was staying was Jasmine so she could cover for me in case my parents called or something."

"So you're not all conspiring to make sure I'm not alone because I'm a danger to myself?" It comes as more of an accusation than a question.

"No one's conspiring anything, Delta." She sneaks another look at me without the lip biting this time. She almost has me convinced until she says, "And even if we were making plans to help you, we'd be doing it as friends."

Chapter 22

I stay quiet the rest of the short ride to the grocery store. Before we even pull in, it's obvious the parking lot is unusually busy for a Friday afternoon.

As we take a right into the lot, an oncoming SUV blows through the intersection and turns left, cutting us off. Emberly slams on the brakes, stopping just short of crashing. She blasts the horn, and the lady driving the SUV flips us off and proceeds into the lot. Emberly's hands shake on the steering wheel as she slowly finds a parking spot far away from the obnoxious SUV lady.

"What is with people and storms?" Emberly's face is all blotchy.

I think the near-miss really got to her, and I feel a sense of protectiveness rise in me. "You okay?"

"Yeah." She forces a smile. "It just got my adrenaline pumping is all."

We grab a stray cart from the lot. Emberly pushes while we head into the store.

She checks her phone. "My mom's sent me a whole list." She turns to me, her face still blotchy. "Sorry, this might take a little longer than expected."

We pass by the freezer that holds the bagged ice, and it's completely empty. "I hope ice isn't on the list."

"It is." She sighs as she types into her phone and I take over pushing the cart. "We'll have to make some at home with the ice maker."

Her phone chimes with a message and Emberly bites her lip in worry while she reads it. I wish she wouldn't do that; it makes me all kinds of distracted, and I'm still trying to be kind-of sort-of mad at her.

"My mom is freaking out. We've never lived this close to the water before." She sighs again. "Let's see if there's any water left."

We manage to get the last two packages of bottled water, some off-brand I've never heard of, but hopefully it'll be good enough for Emberly's mom. As we head down the aisle in one direction, the SUV lady comes up the other way. She doesn't acknowledge us as we walk by, even though she almost killed us. I glance over my shoulder and find to my satisfaction that she's standing by the empty water section, scouring the shelves. I'm tempted to go back and gloat, but Emberly's impatiently waiting for me in the next aisle.

We grab what we can from her mom's list, things like applesauce and bread, but there are a lot of things already out of stock. We fail to get any peanut butter or toilet paper. Though I seriously doubt they're completely out of toilet paper at Emberly's house.

My eyes go wide at the black credit card Emberly uses to pay for everything, including a couple of candy bars we grab at the checkout counter.

She notices my look. "My dad gave it to me for emergencies. I figured this counts."

Of course, I noticed how much bigger Emberly's house is than mine, and how it overlooks the beach. I spent enough time hanging around her this summer to realize her parents clearly have money, way more money than my parents. And she's been driving me around in her expensive car. But it's not until I see that black card that I realize how big the divide is between what my family has and what Emberly's has.

An ungrateful thought goes through my head. When Emberly was in trouble, her parents were able to pay for the help she needed and to move her to a completely new town to start over. If the same thing had happened to me, my parents would be drowning in hospital debt and there would be no money to move away. I saw Gemma's hospital bills after eight days in the hospital. The only reason we didn't have to take out a second mortgage on our house to pay those bills was because so many people gave us money at the funeral. I doubt people would be so generous a second time, and for something like an attempted suicide.

As it is, my parents still owe the lawyers who consulted with us on Gemma's case. I peeked at that bill on my stepdad's dresser the other day. According to the lawyers, there was no cause of a lawsuit based on Gemma's care, despite the mysterious circumstances of her death, but my mom said she had to "make sure my baby was properly taken care of." The lawyers gave her that piece of mind at least...at a cost.

My ugly feelings about being a have-not don't mean I'm not glad that Emberly's okay. She seems totally recovered; I never would have guessed what she had done if she hadn't told me. What I don't get is why everyone doesn't get access to the same resources.

It scares me because I can't forget that peaceful feeling that overcame me when the water rose over my ears. My head was so quiet and calm, in a way it hasn't been since Gemma died. I don't think I would have stayed there and let the water take me if Logan hadn't dragged me out of it, but I kind of wish I had a little more time to feel that peace.

I'm so lost in thought that I hardly notice when Emberly pulls up in front of my house.

"My mom will never let me stay out again tonight," she says, "not with her being paranoid about the storm."

"That's okay. I'll be fine by myself." I say it as if I wasn't just thinking about being underwater.

"I know." Her lips turn down into a pout. "I wasn't thinking about that. I was thinking about last night in your bed."

My body responds to her words with heat and wanting, but my heart still stings over her talking behind my back, whether her concerns were warranted or not.

I nod toward the trunk. "You should get all this stuff home to your mom."

I go to open the door, but Emberly touches my arm. "Wait!" I think maybe she wants to kiss me goodbye, and I'm torn between wanting a kiss so badly it hurts and being sore over the betrayal. "Are you sure you don't want to call Jasmine and stay over there for the weekend?"

So she wants to go down this road again. I pull my arm away and push open the door with more force than necessary then slam it shut behind me. I hear the passenger window go down.

"Delta!" Emberly yells as I stomp away. "Not because I think you're suicidal. I don't think you should be alone during the hurricane."

"Jasmine's going to the party tomorrow night!" I yell. "If I go over there, it'll ruin that for her."

"So go to the party," Emberly pleads. "I'll meet you there."

"Sounds like your mom's not gonna let you out of her sight for the next forty-eight hours."

"I'll find a way to sneak out and meet you there."

"Why not come here then and spend the night with me?"

My phone rings, which gives me an excuse to end this conversation. Every minute I spend with Emberly right now is ruining the good times we had together. All her words have a double meaning, and I can't make sense of her motives.

I pick up the phone. "Hi, Mom. Hang on a sec." I cover the speaker and say to Emberly, "I gotta go. It's my mom calling from Jamaica."

Emberly leans way over the passenger seat. "I'll call you later. I love you, Delta."

I wave noncommittally and put the phone back up to my ear, using it as an excuse not to say "I love you" back. The truth is I don't know how I feel about Emberly right now.

Chapter 23

I half listen to the first part of my mom's conversation while unlocking the door to my house. She's freaking out that the hurricane is coming and she's not here. No surprise there, but I hate that it's ruining her vacation.

"Mom," I try to interrupt her once my backpack is put away, but she's still talking. "Mom!"

That shuts her up, followed by, "You don't have to yell."

Apparently I do, but I don't say that. Giving her attitude won't help. "The storm's not coming until tomorrow. I'll be fine here tonight, and then I'll go to Jasmine's and stay there until it all blows over." The lie comes so easily.

I hear her relaying this information to my stepdad. "I think we should call Cheryl," she says to him.

That's Jasmine's mom, so I immediately say, "You don't have to do that. You can't spend your whole vacation worrying about me." I say it matter-of-factly, like I'm the grown-up in the situation. "Let me talk to Gary." Maybe I can get him to get her to relax about this whole thing.

My stepdad's voice comes through the phone, "Hi, kiddo. Everything okay?"

"Everything's fine." I've lied about that so many times, it's like second nature now. "Can you help her believe that? When are you two ever going to be in the Caribbean again? Make sure she enjoys it."

"We have been. She's just worried, and you can't really expect her not to be."

"I know." And I really do know. When the worst possible thing happens, it makes you worry about it happening again. If one daughter can die, what's to say the other couldn't, too. The impact of Gemma's death on my mom is the biggest reason for me not the let the tide sweep me away; I'd never want to make her experience losing a child again.

"But I'll try to put her mind at ease. It's almost happy hour. We'll go get some of that fine Jamaican rum." There's a teasing tone to his voice, and I hope he really does get my mom drunk. That'll chill her out, and based on how little wine it takes on the rare occasion she has it, a drink or two should do it.

"Thanks, Gary."

"No problem. Take care of yourself, kiddo. We're trusting that you'll be safe and sound when we get back."

He puts my mom back on, and she seems less frantic as we say our goodbyes.

After I get off the call, the house feels unnaturally quiet. I flip on the TV, which is already on the 24-hour news program. It's covering the storm, so I leave it on.

They're showing the path the storm has already taken, and in bright red, the expected future path. A bunch of other possible paths are marked off with lighter red lines, including one that looks like it goes right over my town and another that has the storm taking a right-hand turn out into the Atlantic Ocean.

It's still so far away, it's hard to believe it'll be here tomorrow night...if it comes at all. I'm pulling for it to head out to sea. Let my friends—rather former friends—have their party.

Better yet, let me ignore Gemma telling me to "beware the storm." Let me believe Gemma's ghost is all in my head.

As much as I'm not excited about the idea of imagining things, it's better than the alternative. I shudder to think of Gemma's ghost mouth open in that silent scream. The fear in her eyes when she tried to tell me more. I don't want that for my sister: dead, alive, or a ghost.

The meteorologist drones on about storm surges, rainfall numbers, and expected wind speeds, the voice pulling me out of going too far with the thoughts of Gemma being tortured for all eternity.

"Although mandatory evacuations had previously been issued for North Carolina's Outer Banks, at this time, authorities are recommending anyone who hasn't evacuated to stay put. Most of the bridges have been closed as Ophelia is expected to bring hurricane winds to the area starting in the next few hours."

The constant storm chatter isn't much better than my thoughts. My heart rate jacks up and my throat tightens, like a panic attack is on the way. I switch off the news and put music on instead. Even after a few minutes of relaxing music and breathing exercises, my body is still abuzz with anxious energy. I can't get the image of Gemma's silent scream out of my head.

A run. I need to run.

I quickly change into my running clothes. I lock the door behind me and put my spare key in my shorts pocket because it's easier to keep on me than my whole keychain. I never used to have to worry about locking up for a run. With both of us doing fall sports and having all the same friends, if Gemma was out, I was out.

Now it's glaringly obvious how much my parents aren't home because of work. As the pocket with the key flaps against my leg, I tell myself that at least my parents are gone because they're on vacation and enjoying themselves. I picture my mom in her bathing suit, a flowered wrap tied around her waist, sipping a rum cocktail with one of those umbrellas in it.

The wind blows my ponytail around as I head down my street and take the turns to the one-way beach road about a half mile away. If I take this road to the main road and loop back around to my road, it's about a 3.5-mile run. Hopefully, that will give my anxiety enough time to evaporate. Sometimes I actually can run away from my problems.

Not today, though. By the time I get halfway down the beach road, my breath is more labored than ever. The sky above is blue, but far out over the ocean, bands of white clouds form, an omen of what's to come. A gust of wind shoots sand in my face and steals the last of my breath.

Chapter 24

I stop in the middle of the sidewalk to try and catch my breath, but it's all gaspy heaves. Guess I was wrong when I said I could run away from my problems. I stumble across the beach toward the water and lay down right in the sand but well clear of the temptation of the rising tide.

On one side of my face, the sun is a warm beacon. On the other, the wind stirs up grains of sand to pelt my cheek. I close my eyes and focus on the contrasting sensations on my face, feel the give of the sand beneath my body. Then I listen for the waves, try to match my breathing to the steady in and out of the water.

It sort of works. At least I don't think I'm going to pass out, but my throat remains thick and my chest tight with too little oxygen.

A rumbling sound rolls down from the road, and I sit up as two motorcycles travel side-by-side down the street. They disappear around a bend, though I can hear them drive all the way to the main road where they rev up and rumble loudly away.

My ears ring long after the motorcycles are gone, the whooshing of the waves muted, like they're at the far end of a tunnel.

Then I think I hear my name being called softly.

I search the sidewalk and beach, but no one is near enough to have called my name so softly and have me hear it.

"Delta," the call comes again.

I stand and do a full three-sixty searching for the

source of the call. A gull cries out overhead, but there's no mistaking its distinct squawk for my name.

"Delta."

I rub my ears and stride in the direction I think it's coming from, my sneakers kicking up sand behind me as I move swiftly down the beach.

The soft calls continue, but I never seem to be getting any closer to them. I pick up my pace to a run, awkwardly because my sneakers push deep into the sand with each step as if the beach is reluctant to let me catch my quarry.

I end up running all the way to where the sand turns to small rocks and shells, which crunch under my tread. They are thick with algae and seaweed, so I slow my pace and listen for the call. There is only the wind and the waves. Up ahead is the Sea Glass Lodge.

It's off by itself, the only structure on this part of the coastline. It's three stories tall, and not very expansive. From this angle, it looks a little crooked, ready to succumb to sea if compelled strongly enough. A lone, hunched sentinel standing guard over the water.

Whoever was calling my name has stopped, perhaps having guided me to my destination. Seeing the Sea Glass Lodge, I think of that show where celebrities give viewers tours of their homes. Whenever they get to the bedroom, they say, "This is where the magic happens."

Tomorrow night, this is where my friends will be...if they're allowed out. Do I want to be where the magic happens?

I crunch my way to the Sea Glass Lodge. The front of the house faces the water. It's surrounded by a rocky, shell-filled beach on all sides, and the back leads to a winding, unpaved road. That road will be filled with cars tomorrow night.

The potent stench of low tide blows in the breeze, though the water level looks high. Usually at low tide, sand bars stretch out well into the water, but none are visible right now, so the strong scent is yet another mystery. With the wind in my ears on this remote part of the beach, the whole world outside this space could have evaporated and I would have no idea. As it is, it feels like I could be the only person who exists right now.

Cuts of sunlight peek through the approaching clouds and glint against a large front window that could easily be mistaken for stained glass, but it's actually where the house gets its name. The window is divided into eight evenly-sized panes, each one made of hundreds of pieces of sea glass. The small shards of white, brown, green, and the occasional blue look like the real deal, not the mass-produced stuff sold at beachside gift shops. It's an awful lot of glass to have been collected, the edges pounded smooth by the waves and deposited on the beach as tiny found treasures. It makes me wonder about the person who created this window and what happened to them. No one has lived in this house for as long as I can remember.

Next to the sea-glass window sits the front door, a moldy hunk of wood hanging on by three rusty hinges. A bouquet of buoys hangs on for dear life, faded and dented as if they've endured dozens of hurricanes. A rusted iron pineapple serves as a door knocker, but I don't dare touch it for fear of tetanus. The tarnished metal doorknob appears pristine in comparison, and I risk grabbing it, pressing my thumb on the latch to find the door unlocked. It creaks as I pull it open enough to sneak inside.

The smell of decay is worse inside than outside. A shaft of sunlight makes it through the sea-glass window to give the space a strange, underwater quality, like standing inside an aquarium tank. The air is thick and damp, and there's a faint dripping sound coming from somewhere deep inside the house.

Parker wasn't lying about the kegs already being delivered. Three silver caskets are lined up along the entrance hall. I climb a carpeted staircase to the second floor, the carpet squishy and sandy beneath my feet. At the top of the stairs is a hallway. I slowly walk down it, passing a couple of bedrooms and a bathroom, the doors left open as if waiting for someone to come and live in them. In the deep quietude of the lodge, I can't shake off the feeling of being the only one left in the world.

At the end of the hallway is another stairway leading up to the third floor. This floor is smaller than the others, comprised of a single round room with windows on all sides. I walk around the perimeter, taking in the view from all sides. To the north is the sandy area behind the house. The road disappears into two rows of drooping beetlebung trees. To the west is the river that flows into the Sound and marks the border to the next town over. To the east is the beach near my house, beyond that, too far to see, is the private beach in Emberly's neighborhood. Looking out the south window toward the water is where I stand the longest.

That's when I hear a whisper on the wind. "Delta."

Chapter 25

Long Island Sound isn't like open the ocean with splashing waves and choppy seas. During storms, you might get bigger waves that spray up onto the land, but that's the exception. Rather than crashing, the waters of the Sound ripple with the ebb and flow of the tide. On clear days, the water can be still as glass, a perfect reflection of the world, with Long Island visible out beyond the water, to the point where you can pick out specific buildings.

Today the storm clouds create a dramatic backdrop for Long Island, the land more of a suggestion than a solid presence, a ghost of an island.

My skin is sticky with sweat, but I shiver all the same and pull my gaze away from the gray waters.

There's one more staircase up, a spiraling wrought iron thing, more of a hazard than a viable way to get from one floor to the next. I chance it and make my way up and around to a trapdoor in the ceiling that I have to push on to open. I climb out and carefully lower the trapdoor before standing.

This top floor is open to the elements. It's circular like the floor below but smaller. There is a rickety metal railing all the way around.

I don't know if it's the spiral staircase or the heights, but there's a dizzying quality to this crow's nest. This high up, the wind whips at my hair, smacking the tip of my ponytail against my cheek. It moans in an eerie, humanlike way and dries the sweat off my skin, raising goose bumps.

One of the railing posts rises up higher than the

others as a flagpole. Remnants of a flag that is tattered beyond recognition flap against the pole. Up here, the climate is totally different than at beach level, energetic and hostile.

Despite feeling unmoored, I make my way to the railing and shake it to test its strength. Flakes of rust fly off under my hands, but otherwise, the railing seems sound. I hold on tight and lean over with the top half of my body. The wind picks up, pulling and tearing at my tank top, my shorts flapping hard enough against my legs to sting. A rush of adrenaline shoots through my body. A voice whispers in my head.

Jump. Fly.

A part of me longs to fling a leg over the railing, cling to the outer edge, and lean out as far as I can, hands clinging to the railing my only anchor to this old beach house. To this old life.

The other part of me knows doing things like that is pure madness. It's the kind of thing my friends are all afraid of me doing.

This part of me knows it's cowardly and selfish to risk my life when Gemma no longer has a life to risk. It's not fair to play such games. I have all the chances in the world when she has none. Why would I gamble so foolishly with them?

With all of these thoughts entrenched in my mind, I place the sole of my sneaker on top of the railing, test if it'll hold my weight. The rusty metal is low enough that I can straddle it. I keep one leg on the inside, touching safe ground, and the other leg on the outside, balancing precariously on the lip of the crow's nest.

It makes no sense what I'm doing, but nothing's made sense all summer.

A flash of white out in the water catches my eye. It looks like a person, thrashing around…drowning.

Though no one else is around, I yell, "Help! Somebody help her!"

I can tell it's a girl. Her long, wet hair is matted to her face, obscuring her features. With a desperation to her movements, she swipes at the hair. I can see her clearly; it's Gemma. Gemma is drowning!

My foot perched outside the railing slips. Chunks of the wooden lip crumble under me and nearly send me over the edge. I scramble back to the inside of the crow's nest, falling hard on my backside. Splinters of rusty metal left behind from the railing pierce my hands. Tetanus be damned! I push off the ground and dash to the trapdoor, throwing it open.

Halfway down the spiral staircase, I lose my footing and catch my knee on the metal.

"Fuck!" I hastily rub the spot that is already bruising and limp the rest of the way down, my knee throbbing with each movement. I chance a look out the south window. Gemma still struggles in the water.

I silently will her to hang on as I make my way down the next two flights of stairs, past the kegs in the hallway, and charge out the dilapidated door. I shove it with such force, I'm afraid I'll send it clean off the hinges.

A quick scan of the water shows no signs of Gemma. Not fully stopping, I yank off my sneakers and socks. Then I run toward the water, shells and rocks digging into my feet, drawing blood.

As I wade in, the salt water stings my wounds, and I inhale sharply. At chest level, I let the water take me and dog paddle out to where I think Gemma went down. It's farther out than it looked from up on the crow's nest. The current pulls me too far east. I fight against it to get back to what I think is the right spot, but the sea of gray is far more disorientating than I expected.

I take a deep breath, close my eyes, and dip my head under. I open my eyes to stinging water. All I see is seaweed and murky brown. I try to dive deeper, but it's like fighting a war against myself. My instincts tell me to keep close to the surface, while my panic insists that Gemma's somewhere down here and I have to save her.

Instinct wins, and I come to the surface, spluttering. I try a few more times and find nothing. My legs feel like lead weights trying to sink me. Salt stings my nose and the back of my throat.

Gemma is dead, I remind myself, not out here in the water. The realization hits me like it does each morning. Gemma is gone. I'll never see her again. Or if I do, it'll be her tortured ghost, and that's probably worse than not seeing her.

That's when a wave crashes over my head and sends me under. I take in a big gulp of water, salty and stinging, and lose track of which way is up. Struggling to hold my breath, I flip around like a dying fish and search for the brightest part of the water, the direction that will point me to air and life. Now that it comes down to it, I'm not ready to give up and succumb to the water.

With a desperation to live I didn't think existed in my anymore, I press in what I think...I hope...is the right direction. When I finally surface, I cough, treading water on instinct more than actual skill, until I can breathe again.

I turn toward the coast and find I'm way off from where I started, the Sea Glass Lodge small in the distance. I need to get back to shore before I drown. The thought sends me into a panic spiral. My arms flap uselessly against the surface and my heart thuds in my ears, drowning out the wind and the waves. My muddled brain struggles to recall the techniques to deal with my panic attacks, but I can't remember a single one.

I settle for a simple mantra about swimming that I remember from some kids' movie I watched with Gemma ages ago. In a singsongy voice in my head, I chant to keep swimming. My heavy legs kick and my tired arms move in their stupid dog paddle. Not for the first time, but definitely the most desperately, I lament the fact that I never learned to swim properly.

But I keep swimming. Even as my vision blurs, I pump my legs and paddle my arms. My breaths are gasps, and I try not to suck in water with each one. Just when I think the beach is too far away, that my body will give out, a strange rise in the water propels me forward.

I ride the wave all the way to the shallows where I crawl out of the water and collapse in the sand. It's a long time before I catch my breath and manage to stand up on wobbly legs.

It's an unsteady walk back to the Sea Glass Lodge to retrieve my shoes. Running sneakers are expensive, and my mom will kill me if I leave them at the mercy of the tide. My feet are torn up and my lungs burn from exhaustion and salt water. The walk back home seems impossible, but what other choice do I have?

I didn't bring my phone, so I can't call anyone. There's only Emberly anyway, and I'm not sure how I would explain the state I'm in without freaking her out. My renewed sense of wanting to live propels me forward, one step at a time.

When my mind wanders to the girl in the water crying for help, I remind myself it couldn't have been

Gemma. Dead girls can't drown. I suppose it could have been some other girl, but where would she have come from? And why did I think I could save someone else from drowning when I can't swim?

I send out a desperate prayer that it was only my imagination gone wild because after having almost drowned myself, I wouldn't wish that kind of death on my worst enemy. Well, maybe on Camille, but only if she had something to do with Gemma's death. I'm doubting this harder than ever now, or maybe that's the exhaustion catching up to me. I'll be able to think better when I've rested.

When I finally reach the beach near my house, barely stumbling forward anymore, my thoughts turn to that swell of water that helped me back to shore. It could have been the wake of a boat too far out to see me struggling but sending me a helpful boost all the same.

Or it could have been Gemma's ghost. Maybe my twin-not-twin was out there in the water after all.

Chapter 26

When the phone wakes me on Saturday morning, my mom's screechy and panicked voice comes through loudly. "It's pummeling the Outer Banks! And they're not even getting a direct hit!"

I pull the phone away from my ear and see it's not even 6:30. I fell asleep on Gemma's bed, and the light seeping in through the blinds winks off the jar of sea glass, half blinding me. My sleepy brain is slow to catch on to what my mom is saying.

"The what is what?" I yawn.

"The hurricane!" she practically screams. "It's off the coast of North Carolina right now. I'm watching footage of what's happening there. Ophelia is a category three and is headed right for Connecticut. It's going to be there tonight!"

"Mom—" I begin, but she interrupts.

"There's still time for you to get a bus to your grandmother's. I'll call her now, tell her you're coming."

"No!" I say. There's no way I'm staying with my grandmother and her cats. Gemma and I hated it there as kids. Grandma always made us eat canned vegetables and everything smelled like cat food.

"Emberly and I already picked up water and supplies yesterday." They weren't for me, but my mom doesn't need to know that. "I'll be fine."

"Emberly?" my mom says with surprise. "Aren't you at Jasmine's?"

Shit! I can't remember what I told my mom yesterday. Am I already supposed to be at Jasmine's?

"

"I'm packing my clothes now and heading over there soon." I hope she doesn't call Jasmine's mom because then I'll really have to go there.

"I knew we should have flown home as soon as we heard about this storm." Her voice is muffled, and I think she's talking to my stepdad, not me.

Sure enough, I hear his reply. "It's too late now."

At Gary's prompting, my mom takes a deep breath. "Okay," she says to me. "Head over there soon. They're all talking about how fast this hurricane is moving."

"I will." I consider telling her not to worry if I don't answer my phone once the storm hits because I might lose service, but I think that'll freak her out even more.

"Delta, honey?"

"Yeah, Mom."

"We love you. Stay safe."

"Love you, too."

Fully awake now, I open the blinds to find a gray, swirling sky. Those clouds that were out over the ocean yesterday have arrived. The trees sway in the breeze, but nothing about the weather is particularly unusual for a late-summer morning. It could be a typical stormy day by the beach. It could be, but it's not with Hurricane Ophelia on the way.

Beware the storm.

I can't decide if Gemma's ghost is real or if she's in my head. Either way, I need to set the record straight with Camille. The idea that my sister was poisoned and that Camille was involved has been eroding my sanity. I have to confront her.

As I get out of bed and my feet touch the carpet, I hiss in pain. They are a mess from running barefoot over the rocks and shells outside of the Sea Glass Lodge. I washed and bandaged them last night, but they still smart with every step. I make my way downstairs and pour myself a bowl of cereal with lots of milk. I may as well use up all the perishables with the likelihood of power outages. I'll make sure to eat the rest of the ice cream today.

In an attempt to distract myself from how quiet the house is and how loud my thoughts are, I turn on a playlist I listened to a million times with Emberly this summer. It's all upbeat, fun-at-the-beach music, but it's not enough to keep my thoughts at bay.

What was that out there in the water yesterday? Was someone really calling my name? In the moment, I was convinced there was a girl in the water, and then I was positive it was Gemma. I don't know when I lost the ability to trust what I see, but it's making it difficult to trust anything...or anyone.

And then there's the way I've been treating Emberly. She told me her worst secret and all I did was think about how it affected me. I was so worried about her judging me that I never stopped to make sure she's okay. When really, she was just worried about me, and I should have been worried about her.

Suddenly the kitchen feels too cold. I drop my spoon in what's left of the milk and wrap my arms around me in a kind of self-hug. Even though my feet are sore, I pace the kitchen to try and warm myself, the upbeat music mocking my mood. I should apologize to Emberly, that's what I should do. But first I should make sure everything in the house is in order.

I crank up a new playlist, one of my running ones with lots of loud rock and heavy metal. I use my headphones, even though I'm alone, and it effectively drives out the intrusive thoughts. Then I get to work, loading and running the dishwasher, vacuuming all the carpeted rooms, including my parents' bedroom, and putting on a load of laundry.

When I'm done inside, I slip on a pair of loose sandals, which is about all my feet can tolerate right now, and head outside. There's not much I can do out here, except to check for anything that might blow away. The wind has picked up, and my hair whips around my face as I look around. There's not much in the yard, so I settle for pulling the stained umbrella out of the patio table and putting it in the shed. I notice the grill next to the shed, so I wheel that in as well.

Back inside, I remove the bandages from my feet, opting for the satisfying pain of a quick pull on each one. The playlist goes back on my portable speakers while I shower, scrubbing my feet, almost relishing in the pain of it because I like feeling something other than the storm of grief and doubt churning inside me. The worst of the wounds get repatched after my shower, and then there's only one thing left to do. I'm afraid if I don't do it now, I'll chicken out.

It's not terribly early anymore, so I take a chance that Emberly is awake. For comfort, I rub my hand over the afghan on my bed as I hit the call button.

She picks up after two rings. "Hey, Delta."

"Hey," I say and hesitate.

"Everything okay?"

The question almost makes me clam up, like she's asking because she assumes I'm a mess. I hate that this is her default way of thinking about me. But it's not exactly wrong. I've pretty much been a mess since we met, definitely since we started dating. I remind myself she's asking because she cares. She must care, otherwise she wouldn't have stuck around this long.

"It's just..." Knowing what I want to say and actually saying it are two different things. "I wanted to say I'm sorry."

"Oh." She says it softly, like she can't figure out why I'd be apologizing.

"You told me something really important and hard to admit. And then I got mad about things that have to do with me, not you. And I wanted to apologize and make sure you are good."

"Oh," she says again.

Before my thoughts spiral, I blurt out, "What I mean is, are you okay? You don't feel like..." I'm not sure what the right term is to use. "Hurting yourself anymore, do you?"

"Oh," she says for a third time, but this one has a knowing ring to it. "No, I don't want to hurt myself. I have better tools now, so I can get help if I ever feel that way again."

The conversation feels like it's going to turn to her asking me the same thing I just asked her, and I'm afraid that'll just make me angry again, so I steer it in another direction. "I've been thinking about the party tonight."

"Oh yeah?" Emberly says.

"Is it still on? The storm's supposed to hit pretty hard tonight."

Emberly laughs, and I love the sound of it. It makes me wish she were here with me, so I could find all her ticklish spots and make her laugh again.

"Parker is determined to have this party. Everyone's making plans and saying they're staying at everyone else's houses in order to go because no parent in their right mind is letting their kid go to a party tonight."

She doesn't mention Camille and Jasmine by name, but I'm assuming the "everyone" she's talking about includes them. And that means she's been talking to them, but that doesn't mean she's been talking to them about me, so I remind myself there's no reason to be mad at her.

"What about your parents?" I ask. "Are they letting you go to a sleepover?" A gust of wind rattles the tree branches against the glass of my bedroom window as if to punctuate all the reasons Emberly's parents shouldn't let her out.

She sighs. "Not yet, but I might be able to convince them that the swim team is all staying together tonight."

Again, she doesn't mention Camille and Jasmine, but I'm sure it's one of their houses she would pretend to stay at. I tell myself it's fine for her to use them as a way to get out with me. I'm using Jasmine as a way to appease my mom.

"I'd like to go to the party with you if you can convince your parents to let you."

"I'd love that." I almost tell her I love her, but then she says, "I better go and talk to my mom before the weather gets bad. I'll call you later."

Now to figure out how to fill my time until I hear back from Emberly.

Chapter 27

I'm not holding out much hope that Emberly will be allowed to come over, so that means I have to face the prospect of the rest of the day alone in this tomb of a house. And maybe much longer than that if the storm conditions get bad.

My mom's car is here, but with only a permit, I can't drive myself anywhere, not that I have anywhere to go.

It's so quiet here, even with the increasing wind making its presence known outside. I need a distraction. I turn on the TV, but nothing keeps my attention. I leave the weather coverage on in the background, and meteorologist Kate Jenson drones on about barometric pressure and storm surge. They're now almost certain the storm is headed straight for Long Island before barreling into Connecticut; it's only a matter of which towns will get hit the worst. The storm is moving fast, the eye expected to hit right around midnight. I can't listen to this, so I turn it off.

Why hasn't Emberly gotten back to me?

I contemplate my situation over a half-gallon of rocky road, even though marshmallows aren't really my thing. It was Gemma's favorite. My mom keeps buying it, out of habit I guess, and I keep eating it. I don't have the heart to tell her I don't like it.

The ice cream makes me feel bloated, and my ears feel weird, too, like they have to pop. With the oppressive silence inside the house, it's like being underwater. Which makes me think about struggling for breath. I empty the dishwasher to keep myself away from such thoughts. I'd almost welcome a visit from Gemma's ghost, but there is exactly zero supernatural activity going on right now... unless you count the moaning of the wind.

Maybe with the storm almost here, she feels like she's done all she can by warning me. Or maybe the whole damn thing was in my head in the first place. And Gemma's ghost was a figment of my imagination, a manifestation of the grief and anxiety I've been carrying around for months. I contemplate telling someone about it.

What happens to people who have hallucinations? I'm pretty sure it's not like what happens in the movies, certainly not like the old Jack Nicholson movie based on the book "One Flew Over the Cuckoo's Nest." We were supposed to read it for class last year, but Jasmine didn't want to, so we watched the movie. Doctors don't electroshock patients anymore, do they?

It's not lost on me that Emberly might know something about this. Not that I'm planning on telling her.

And Gemma's ghost seems to be staying away. Real or not, her visit forced me to focus in on Camille's shady behavior. I should confront Camille...tonight at the party. But maybe there's no point to that because it's not like she'd tell me the truth. I should just stay home. If Emberly is allowed out, we can snuggle in bed while the wind howls outside and forget everything but ourselves under the covers.

My mind has been as changeable as a chameleon on a pride flag, but it's time to make a decision.

I have to find out the truth, even if I have to trick it out of Camille. My best bet for doing that is at the party where everyone will be drinking and smoking and her guard will be down. It'll be too hard to get there, though, without Emberly.

Why hasn't she called me back?

For a moment, I consider calling Jasmine and apologizing. I think her happiness over me actually wanting to go out would outweigh her anger over all the shit we've been going through. Then I think of her picking Camille over me. It all comes down to Camille, to whether or not she poisoned Gemma. I have to get to that party tonight.

I can't stay in this house while I wait to hear from Emberly. My twitchy limbs are itching for another run, but my feet are slathered in antibacterial cream and bandages and definitely can't handle a run.

I pace the living room, my stomach rumbling. A loud burp erupts from my mouth and tastes like rocky road. Ugh. Why did I eat so much ice cream?

My feet will have to deal with a walk to the beach. I put on loose sandals, make sure my phone ringer is turned up, and head out. The air is thick and tangible, like I could reach out and grab a handful. No precipitation yet, but I can feel it building in the clouds, ready to burst. The wind does nothing to dissipate the heaviness of the atmosphere. The pressure builds beyond my ears and goes into my head. I rub my temples, but it does little to relieve the pain.

Beware the storm.

The thought plagues me all the way down my road, around the block, and to the beach. The white-capped waves are gray and angry, throwing spray into the air when they hit the concrete fishing pier that juts twenty feet beyond the water line. I stay off the beach because of my bandaged feet and keep to the sidewalk. There are a decent amount of people out walking, probably checking out the beach before Hurricane Ophelia arrives in full.

Beware the storm.

I rub my temples again, this time in an attempt to get

the thought out of my head. It was all in my head, I tell myself. It was never a warning from Gemma; it was a warning from my own subconscious. But if that is true, then wouldn't that mean my own subconscious is warning me about the storm? It's telling me that going to the party tonight is a mistake. That can't be right either.

I reach the point where the beach road turns toward the main road and the sidewalk ends, so I turn around and head back the way I came. I barely register the worsening conditions, a spatter of rain finally joining the wind.

I have to go to his party. I have to see Camille's reaction to Gemma's—my—accusations. It's the only way to know for sure.

I walk up and down that stretch of sidewalk along the beach until my feet are sore and blood begins to soak through parts of the bandages. The wind has picked up, gusting enough to billow out my tank top and fling my ponytail in all directions. Salty spray blows up from the water, mixing with the rain.

No one else is out walking now, everyone gone away to the safety of their homes.

Beware the storm.

My phone beeps with a notification. Two texts come in from Emberly.

> They're letting me out!!!
> Picking up food. Be there in 30

I send back three heart emojis. Then I let out a whoop of joy that gets caught up in the wind. A sizzling streak of lightning rips from the clouds over the Sound and down to the water. It's followed by a deep, rumbling roll of thunder. Being out here feels wild and reckless. I hold my face to the sky and taste the saltiness of the rain.

A grin slides across my face, the first real one I've had in a long time. My restlessness has finally dissipated. Emberly is on her way. We're going to the party. I'm going to find out the truth about Gemma's death tonight one way or another.

Chapter 28

The rain falls harder, sideways at times as the wind blows, soaking my phone screen. I'm soaked through as well and want another shower before Emberly arrives. Better shower while I can. That thought propels me home as quickly as my poor feet will allow.

I'm clean and dressed in a fresh tank top and comfy shorts when Emberly arrives. I open the door to wild weather. The sky is prematurely dark with strange purple-blue clouds. It's raining harder than ever, splatters coming from all directions.

Emberly's dark hair flies around her face. She has a duffel bag and a reusable grocery bag over one shoulder and several paper bags in her hands. I grab the paper bags and quickly usher her in.

"I hope Chinese is okay." She stands in the entryway shivering. "Everything else was closed."

"Perfect," I say. "Let me get you a towel."

My cleaning spree from earlier means there are plenty of fluffy, dry towels in the dryer, something that's been noticeably absent in my life lately. A pang of longing and loss shoots through me as I realize it was my mom who used to make sure we had clean towels and bed sheets and that my cross country uniform was washed before meets. That's the type of thing she hasn't paid much attention to since Gemma died. I guess things like laundry becomes unimportant when your life falls apart. The problem is all our lives have been falling apart and we still need clean towels. I've lost so much more than my sister.

I inhale the fresh scent and let out a long exhale to try and ground myself back into reality. Emberly is here, wet and shivering, and waiting for me to bring her a towel. I find her in the kitchen and try not to stare as she rubs her face, arms, and legs dry. To distract myself from the temptation of Emberly's bare skin, I line up the four containers of food on the counter next to paper plates.

"Help yourself," I say after she's done drying off.

We pile our plates with fried rice, pork, and spring rolls. There are plenty of soy sauce packets, too, because Emberly knows I like it. My house is nearly empty of food, so I don't know what I would have eaten tonight if Emberly hadn't come over. Or for that matter, what I'll eat for the next few days if I can't get to the store.

"I snuck some water and food out of my house for you." She points to the grocery bag she brought, which is sitting on the floor near the fridge. "We had way more than we needed."

I'm reminded that Emberly's been taking care of me. She'd keep track of the laundry for me if I asked her to; she'd probably set a reminder on her phone and everything.

Emberly picks up a fortune cookie and pulls apart the plastic wrapper. She always starts with the fortune. She reads the words on the little strip of paper aloud, "Love is like a sweet nectarine, good to the last drop." She smiles like the thought of someone loving her—of me loving her— is the most pleasing thing in the world. "Your turn."

My fortune is tucked in tight, and the cookie breaks when I tug on the paper. It feels like a bad luck omen. I unfold the paper and immediately see "Beware the storm."

I shriek and drop the slip of paper on my plate.

"What's the matter?" Emberly's gaze darts around, searching for the reason for my reaction, because normal people clearly don't shriek at silly fortunes.

"Sorry," I say quickly. "I hurt my foot yesterday and must have stepped on it wrong."

Emberly gives me a piercing look but doesn't question my excuse, though we both know I was standing still a moment ago. Unfortunately, my explanation brings her attention to my bandaged feet, which I was hoping she wouldn't notice because I know I'll have to make up a story about the wounds.

"What happened?" Emberly asks.

I shrug. "I went barefoot in the water yesterday and stepped on some shells."

"You went in the water by yourself again?" she asks carefully. Then she puts a mouthful of pork and rice in her mouth.

"Just my feet," I lie. "I got really sweaty on my run and thought it might help me cool down."

She forces a smile and gestures to the fortune. "What's it say?"

With dread, I look down at my plate. Soy sauce seeps into the paper, but I can still make out the words. "Your life is what your thoughts make it."

Not what I thought I saw. Another case of my mind conjuring things?

Emberly and I are quiet as we eat. I contemplate the actual fortune. Given where my thoughts have been lately, it's not great. I crumple the paper and drop the tiny ball onto the counter. Emberly takes another bite of spring roll and chews thoughtfully. I've hardly taken a bite, the fortune having ruined my appetite.

This isn't how I wanted the evening to go at all. It was supposed to be about me and Emberly having fun until we headed to the party.

A particularly loud gust of wind rattles the house. We both look at the kitchen window. It's gotten dark enough that it's hard to see anything but the reflection of the bright kitchen lights.

Emberly looks to me with wide eyes. "It's getting kind of nasty out there."

"I'm surprised your mom let you out. You must have had a great reason to convince her."

"Hmmm" is all she says, her gaze fixed on the window as if the storm is a bigger concern than she's let on. I want to kiss the worry off her face. I want to lose myself in her, forget about the storm outside and the one inside myself.

"We don't have to go to the party." I half mean it. Now that Emberly and I are here and alone, and conditions are worsening, I'd be fine with staying home. I could confront Camille another time. The earlier, urgent need for answers is replaced by a different need for Emberly. As long as she's here with me, I don't have to worry about anything else.

I caress Emberly's cheek with my thumb, pulling her from her reverie. Her gaze is no less intense, but not as pensive, as it switches from the window to me.

"We could have our own party of two here," I say, and that brings a smile to her face.

"That would be nice." She takes my hand from her face and kisses each one of my fingers. "I think we should go, though. It'll be good to get out."

"If you say so." My hunger for Emberly outweighs my hunger for food. I pull her close and kiss her. She tastes of soy sauce and a hint of orange, though I don't think there's any orange in the food. We end up on the couch in the living room and forget about dinner and the party while we get lost in each other again.

Chapter 29

So lost in our own world together, Emberly and I barely notice the hurricane raging outside. We haven't bothered to turn on any lights in the living room, and the only time the storm makes its presence known is when the lights in the other room flicker off and on a couple of times.

Eventually, we come up for air and cuddle on the couch. My stomach grumbles, right underneath where Emberly's head is resting, and she giggles.

"I guess we should finish dinner and get ready." She checks her phone and I can't help but see she has a bunch of new text messages, the most recent of which is from Jasmine.

Maybe it's time to try and make up with my best friend. It would certainly make things less awkward with Emberly since she's close with Jasmine. A pang of despair steals my breath for a moment when I, once again, think about all the things Gemma is missing out on, of all the things I've lost without her.

If Gemma were still here, she would be friends with Emberly. Jasmine and I wouldn't be fighting. Logan would still be with Gemma, and there would be no reason to confront Camille, to wonder if she poisoned my sister. There would be no ghost Gemma to haunt my waking and sleeping hours.

Instead of being madly in love and telling Gemma all about it, I ache with sadness every day. I can't fully enjoy this new love. The storm sucks away at my insides, tearing me apart but also leaving no room for the good feelings.

Jasmine and I call each other best friends, but we know it's a lie. We both know Gemma was my first best friend, and I'm struggling to stay above water without her here.

"Hey," Emberly says, her phone now dark. "You okay?"

I shake my head out of my funk. "Yeah. Just hungry."

We heat up our abandoned Chinese food and quickly eat. The hurricane is a somber soundtrack to our hasty meal. Then it's time to get ready for the party.

I poke my head out the front door, only to be confronted with a face full of blowing rain. We don't bother with touching up our makeup, there's no point when it would get washed away the instant we stepped outside. No waterproof mascara can stand up to Hurricane Ophelia.

Emberly brought rain boots, yellow ones with white ducks, and they are as adorable as she is. I pull out my plain black boots, along with a black rain jacket. I mix up my monochrome outfit with bright pink shorts that barely poke out from underneath my jacket. Emberly teases me that all the girls will try to steal me away, but I can barely manage a half-hearted smile in return.

A whistling outside, followed by the rattle of the windows, an ominous reminder of what we're headed into. It's not only the weather but confronting Camille as well. My feet are getting colder by the minute about this party, and I haven't even stepped out into the storm yet.

"I'm not sure too many people are going to come tonight. You're sure you want to go?"

Emberly bites her bottom lip. "We should go." Her determination makes me uneasy, like there's something suspicious behind it, but I chalk the feeling up to nerves. I still have no idea what I'm going to say to Camille, whether

I'll try to trick her into talking or whether I'll outright ask her about Gemma.

Emberly failed to pack a jacket and her sweatshirt would be soaked through before we'd make it to the car, so I do something I never would have been able to do two months ago. I lend her one of Gemma's jackets. It's yellow with buttons that look like hooks. With her hood on, Emberly resembles a fisherman, only the sexiest fisherman I've ever seen.

When we head out to the car, the wind is whipping worse than ever but the rain has let up a bit. Still, Emberly turns her wipers all way on high and the defrost up to keep the windshield clear. The night is dark, and I'm thankful for high beams. We have to dodge a few fallen branches on the side roads, but otherwise, our path is clear.

That is until we get to the dirt road that leads to the Sea Glass Lodge. Emberly stops the car a few feet after making the turn. Standing water blocks our way.

"Do you think it's safe?" she asks.

Lacking a driver's license, I'm certainly not an expert on the rules of the road. I think I remember reading about not driving through water if you can't tell how deep it is, but I'm not sure.

I unbuckle my seatbelt. "I'll take a look."

The wind makes it hard to open the car door, but I manage to push it open. I brace myself against the elements and step out into a muddy mess of a road. I think the conditions have gotten worse since we left my house. I find a long stick, wade in a few inches, and poke the stick as far into the middle of the water as I can reach. It goes down farther than I'd hoped. I toss the stick and head back to the car a little out of breath from the wind beating down on me. Emberly is texting someone when I slide back into my seat, water dripping everywhere. She hastily puts her phone in the cup holder and fiddles with her woven bracelet.

"I think we can make it." My body is buzzing, eager to get to the party or maybe it's just overstimulated from my time with Emberly and the beating from the storm. Either way, I want to get to that party. Emberly's SUV is big and sturdy, I'm almost positive we'll be fine.

"Okay," she says. She backs up a few feet to get a good running start. Then she guns it, shouting, "Here we go!"

The tires spin in the mud and then lurch the car forward as they catch purchase, my body also lurching forward as far as the seatbelt will allow. We hit the water and it splashes up the side of the car in a wave action. The car slips sideways, the headlights pointing at the beetlebung trees that line the road, but Emberly turns the wheel to correct our course.

We careen through the water, both of us screaming. I close my eyes and hope Emberly has the sense to keep hers open. We're hydroplaning and slipping sideways again. Then there's a bump that forces my eyes open. The tires find solid ground, and Emberly slows the car.

She puts it in park and turns on an interior light. Her eyes are wide and her cheeks are flush.

With a hand on her heart, she smiles and whoops. "We made it!"

I lean across and kiss her, adrenaline pumping through me. "You are amazing."

Before we get carried away, I lean back into my seat.

"You ready to party?" she asks, her eyes bright.

"I'm ready to party!" I shout.

Emberly turns off the inside light, and it's an uneventful rest of the drive to the Sea Glass Lodge. As we park next to our classmates' cars and lights from the house peek through the driving wind and rain, I can't help but think our ride over here was nothing compared to what this party has in store for us.

Chapter 30

I don't know who had the foresight to prepare a fire in the Sea Glass Lodge's fireplace—I can't imagine Parker masterminding more than the kegs—but it's a welcome sight as we drip and shiver into the house. We stand in front of the flames and warm ourselves, me rubbing the feeling back into my cold hands. Despite the tropical nature of the hurricane, it's bringing a lot of cold rain. Or maybe it's the wind that makes everything feel cold.

If I thought my house sounded rickety in the storm, it's nothing compared to the beating this old lodge is taking. There's a constant rattling and moaning that can be heard over the pumping music coming from somewhere upstairs. Down here, it's just me, Emberly, and a moldy couch. There was only one keg in the hallway when we came in, so two must have been moved upstairs.

Emberly coughs and rubs her eyes. "The fire's a little smoky."

Now that she mentions it, there is a sort of haze in the room. A giant gust of wind whistles like a teakettle boiling over. The flames gutter and the fire almost goes out. Emberly clutches my arm, and I hold her tight right back.

"Shit," she says with a nervous laugh. "That was a big one." Her phone buzzes with a text, but she quickly flicks the notification away. I'm trying not to be annoyed with the constant texting, the wondering about who's she talking to...whether it's about me. I'm trying.

My hands are thawing out, so I'm ready. Though, I'm not quite ready to confront Camille. I'm still mulling over what to say. And I'd like a little liquid courage before I have that conversation.

"Let's get a drink," I suggest.

Emberly nods, so it's into the tempest we go.

As soon as we reach the hallway on the second floor, it's clear this is not the party floor. Another flight of stairs takes us to the party floor, the circular room with all the windows. Any other night and this would be the place I would want to party, but tonight, with the wind churning and the rain pelting the windows, it's freaky up here.

Since there's no electricity at the Sea Glass Lodge, the room has been lit with candles and large flashlights that stands upright. A battery-charged disco ball sits in the middle of the room, adding a clublike quality. With the myriad of lights and faces reflecting off the windows, it's like the room itself is moving. Loud music pulses all around the room. It's a sensory overloading experience.

I squint and try to get my bearings. Among the dozen or so people here—the ones brave, or stupid, enough to come out tonight—Jasmine comes into focus first. When she spots me, she squeezes between me and Emberly and flings an arm around each of us.

"You made it!" Her words are slurred, and her body leans heavily on me. Clearly she started partying early, and clearly she's forgotten or no longer cares about our fight.

"We did." Emberly shoots me a nervous glance, but there's no reason for that because I'm not here to pick a fight with Jasmine. I've got a bigger ship to sink in Camille.

"So that story about the dedication worked on your mom?" Jasmine says.

"What dedication?" I pose the question more to Emberly than Jasmine.

Emberly rolls her eyes like she has no idea what

Jasmine is talking about. "Nothing. Never mind." She looks distracted as she checks her phone again.

"Come on. The drinks are over here." Jasmine half-guides, half-falls to where two kegs stand. A smattering of hard liquor bottles, sodas, and red cups are set up on the floor next to them.

Parker's there, lording over the kegs, like they're loyal subjects. Like a true lord, Parker's going to pump them dry by the end of the night. "What'll it be, party goddesses?"

I take a cup of beer, and Emberly pours a rum and coke. I quickly down half my cup when I spot Logan and Camille rowdily dancing across the room. They're with a few other seniors, all from the swim team. A group of juniors, also mostly on the swim team, head over to the kegs. They say "hi" while Parker serves them.

There are a lot of "Delta, good to see you" type comments. I've seen them all at school this week, but it's been a while since I've made an appearance at a social function. Since the last party Gemma attended, in fact. I'm grateful for Emberly's hand in mine, a warm security blanket entwined in my fingers.

Then she pulls it away to check her phone again. I'm about to ask Emberly what is up with her phone when Jasmine grabs my hand and pulls me to an open space. She wraps her arms around my neck and rests her forehead against mine.

"Can we stop fighting now?" she asks loudly enough to be heard over the music, which somebody just turned up. It's so loud, I can't hear the hurricane raging outside.

"Sure." I'm hurt that she doesn't understand about the way I've been acting, but I don't think she will ever truly understand my feelings, so there's no point in being mad about it. Plus, I miss the only best friend I have left, and I can't rely on Emberly for all the friend stuff when she already does so much in the girlfriend department.

"Really?" Jasmine shrieks, and I nod. "Yay!"

She jumps up and down, spilling half her drink on the floor, not that she notices. Her enthusiasm is contagious. I'm tired of being sad all the time. The room is electric, and I let it energize me. I down the rest of my drink and get another one.

Emberly joins us, and the three of us form our own dance circle. Another song starts up, the deep beat pulsing in my body. We drink and dance as song after song plays. Then we drink and dance some more.

A joint gets passed our way, and I take a couple of hits. I'm having so much fun, the reason I originally came to this party is a distant memory. Maybe the storm washed away that depressed girl from the summer. Now I can be the Delta who remembers how to have fun. For a second, I forget about why I was sad in the first place, the storm of grief silent for once.

That lasts until Camille crosses the room and breaks into our circle. That's all it takes for the temporarily dormant rain clouds inside me to burst. Every bad feeling from the last two months comes rushing back. They hit like a 100-mph wind and suddenly I can't breathe. The grief storm churns up with renewed energy.

And it's not because I forgot Gemma was dead; there's no forgetting that. It's because, for a moment, I didn't care that she was...I was having fun anyway.

Chapter 31

Camille is in between Jasmine and Emberly, directly across from me. When the song ends, there's a moment where I stare her down, her smile wavering under my glare.

She breaks eye contact and looks from Emberly to Jasmine, the grin returning in full force. "Is everyone enjoying the dedication ceremony for Gemma's plaque?"

"What?" I ask as the next song loudly pumps through the speakers. I turn to Emberly and shout, "What did she say about Gemma?"

Emberly opens her mouth, but nothing comes out.

"What is she talking about?" I screech.

Still, Emberly has nothing to say, just a panicked look as she reaches for me. I step back out of her reach and think back on all the messages she's been getting, and the secretive demeanor I told myself I was imagining. But I wasn't imagining it; Emberly and Camille have been up to something.

I charge over to Parker. "Turn off the music!"

They react quickly under my command, reaching into their pocket, pulling out a phone, and tapping on the screen. Despite the racket of the wind, rain, and crashing waves outside, in an instant, the room feels very quiet. Now everyone else is aware something is up, and all eyes turn to me. They belong to people Gemma cared about: her boyfriend, her best friend, her teammates. Every single person in this room was closely connected to Gemma in some way. Even Emberly, clinging to Jasmine in a way that says she knows she did something wrong, is here because of

Gemma, because of her connection to Gemma through me.

A building rage obscures any embarrassment I might have felt about the attention, something that's been hard to deal with since Gemma died. Everyone knows I'm the girl with the dead sister, a death that might not have been from a mysterious illness but intentional. And everyone here, including the one person who I thought was looking out for me, is in on the secret. The storm I've been holding back all this time, the one always churning deep within me, rages to get out. I'm tired of keeping it at bay. I'm ready to unleash it and drown everyone around me.

"What did you say about Gemma?" I spit the words at Camille.

"We all told our parents we're putting a plaque at the pool in memory of Gemma tonight. That's why we all were allowed to come out." Camille gestures around the room, and I look around at all the faces of Gemma's friends and see betrayal in every single one. "Our parents think we're at the school, being supervised by the swim coaches." Camille glances between me and Emberly with a question in the tilt of her eyebrows. "Didn't Emberly tell you?"

"No, Emberly did not tell me." I enunciate each word carefully.

The spinning lights of the disco ball swirl across their faces, the light dancing to the soundtrack of the storm with the music silenced.

"We really did get a plaque," Camille says as if that's what's concerning me. "And we are going to put it at the pool, just not tonight."

Logan has made his way across the room and is standing protectively next to Camille as if she needs protection. Where was he when Gemma needed protecting?

Jasmine attempts a smile. "C'mon, Delta. Let's put

the music back on and dance some more. Gemma would've wanted you to have fun tonight, not mope around like you've been doing all summer."

As if echoing the turbulent storm taking over my body, a huge gust of wind shakes the whole house. A loud boom sounds from somewhere in the distance and a weird sort of energy travels through the house.

Logan looks at his phone. "Service is down. I bet the power's out. Not that it matters here."

I barely hear him. I'm stuck on the fact that everyone in this room is using Gemma's death as an excuse to be here. That's why we're all here having fun at a party and not safe at home, because Gemma is dead. Only no one bothered to tell me, and now I'm part of dishonoring Gemma's memory.

My rage turns on Emberly. "That was your excuse to your mom! So when you said you had no idea what Jasmine was talking about earlier, you were lying?"

"Delta—" she tries to say, but I cut her off.

"No. I don't want to hear it. And you," I point at Camille. "I can't believe you, of all people, would use Gemma's name to plan this whole thing."

"What's that mean?" Camille presses her hands to her hips and narrows her eyes. "She was my best friend! You don't own the memory of her."

"She was *my* best friend!" I yell. I'm not so consumed by the storm to miss Jasmine's hurt look at my declaration. But she's always known how it stood with me and Gemma; everyone else was second.

I'm determined to unleash this storm on Camille now that I've started. If I've been waiting all this time for the right moment to confront her, this is it. "You have no right to make any claims on Gemma when you had something to do with her death."

"What are you talking about?" Camille splutters. "Me having something to do with Gemma's death. That's insane! How dare you say that."

Logan knits his eyebrows in concern and puts an arm around Camille, who's crying. "Delta," he says carefully, like he's trying to coax a scared kitten out of hiding, "Gemma got sick. How could Camille have anything to do with that?"

"It was the pathologist who did Gemma's autopsy," I explain calmly. Now that I've released the poison of what Gemma's ghost told me, the wind and flood of emotions inside me have dissipated, like the storm of grief has finally subsided. "She said Gemma's lungs were so bad, they looked like she'd been poisoned."

"That doesn't mean that's what happened to Gemma." Tears shine in Logan's eyes, but he has no right to be sad when he's standing there defending the person who betrayed Gemma the minute her body turned cold. "It's tragic what happened to Gemma, and that you and your family—none of us—got any good answers about what made her sick, but you can't really think Camille poisoned her."

Everyone's staring at me like I'm paranoid. They're trying to make me doubt myself. But they weren't there when the pathologist said it looked like poison. They weren't there when the lawyers and the third-party doctors they hired grilled my parents with questions about Gemma, asking if she was sexually active, wanting to know every detail of her life and of that last party we went to. They weren't there when Gemma's ghost showed up, silently screaming.

Emberly reaches out and touches my arm, but the

contact burns my skin. I see the judgment in her eyes, but she's the one who lied to me.

They're all judging me, and they're all liars. Medical freaking mystery, my ass! Gemma's death was no mystery; she was murdered. And they're all in on it...or they're all in denial. Either way, I don't need to stay here and be around these fools.

"I'm out of here!" I head for the stairs and run down them two at a time. A trample of footsteps follow me.

"Wait!" Emberly yells. I stumble on the second set of stairs and she catches up to me. She presses her fancy SUV key fob into my hand. "Take my car. And drive safely, please."

I stop and look at her, see the pity in her expression. We've caused a bottleneck on the stairs with Camille, Logan, and Jasmine all right behind Emberly. Their expressions mirror hers. They all feel sorry for me, but is it because my sister is dead or because they've been keeping the truth of her death a secret from me?

I close my hand in a tight fist around the key fob. Without a word, I take the last few stairs to the first floor and fly to the door. I barely have to grasp the handle and push when the wind does the work of ten of me and flings it open. The old door can't handle the impact, and one of the rusty hinges fails, leaving the door to flap uselessly in the wind. I leave it all behind and step out into the wild hurricane.

Within seconds, I'm fully immersed in the storm. Though the Sea Glass Lodge is only feet away, it's hard to see through the rain that seems to come from all directions. Lightning flashes over Long Island Sound, illuminating the dangerous clouds above and the swirling waters below. If my friends are shouting for me to come back, I can't hear them over the roar of the storm. I put my hands over my ears, not that it helps, and push against the wind toward Emberly's car, or at least in the direction I think it's in. It's hard to tell up from down in this weather.

Water sloshes over my boots. I'm so soaked and the wind makes it so hard to walk that I didn't notice I'm knee-deep in a puddle. More than a puddle, more like a flowing river. I'm deep enough that the current pulls at me. I struggle to keep my balance.

I trudge in deeper, determined not to let a little water keep me from getting away from these liars. Lightning flashes nearby. There's a sizzling sound. The smell of ozone mixes with the salty tang of the water.

A gust of wind sweeps around me. It pushes up through my clothes and billows them out like I'm a hot air balloon. The air current unbalances me as the water current tugs at my boots.

I lose my balance and fall backward into the rogue river. Water streams over my face. I splutter, my hands flailing, trying to find purchase in the slippery silt beneath me.

In my struggle, I forget to hold my breath and inhale. Buckets of water fill me. My body grows heavy.

Gemma's face appears in my spotty vision. She opens her mouth and says, "Delta," like she's welcoming me home.

I stop struggling and surrender to the water.

I'm coming, Gemma.

It's the last thought I have before my senses dull and my vision turns black.

Chapter 32

I'm swimming in a swirling ocean of color. Me—swimming a perfect breaststroke. I laugh at the absurdity of finally being able to swim after always being surrounded by swimmers and never being able to do it myself. The laugh echoes all around me, vibrating through the swirls in a way that I can see.

The echoing laughs are as contagious as real laughs, the kind that roll of out control until tears stream down your face and you can hardly breathe.

Breathe. Breathe. I can't.

The laughs turn to gasps, deep, heaving inhalations in an attempt to fill my lungs with air. But I can't fill lungs that I don't have. I look down and find I have no body; it's only swirling colors. They grow and shrink with my desperate attempts to breathe, like they are me, and we're dying.

A harsh pain thuds my back, or where my back would be if I had one. Then it burns where my throat should be.

Big, bright stars replace the swirls. I open my eyes...I have eyes! And a body! An aching body that's hunched over and shaking with chills, shuddering with coughs that feel like they're tearing apart my insides and sending them out my mouth.

"Breathe, Delta, breathe," someone says.

People keep telling me to breathe as if it's something that requires effort and not a thing my body is supposed to do automatically. I guess since Gemma died, breathing has been something that's required effort.

A hand smacks me on my back and I choke up water, just a small amount, though it feels like it's gutting me. After a moment, I find I can inhale, the oxygen filling me, taking away some of the pain. The next time I exhale, only air comes out. I must have purged all the water.

It takes me that long to remember storming out of the house, attempting to wade through the rushing waters, and falling, struggling, giving up.

Somehow I'm back in the house in front of the smoky fire. Arms wrap around me and the caustic scent of too much cologne surrounds me.

"Fuck, Delta," says Logan near my ear. "You gotta stop doing shit like this."

"I fell," I say through a scratchy throat.

"And the other night you were just lying in the water for fun?" Logan holds me at arm's length, the full heat of his classic good-boy looks on me. While they captivated Gemma, they do little to stir any kind of desire in me. Now, all they stir up is guilt because Logan's question has hit on the turmoil deep in my soul. "You can't do that to Gemma."

"Do what?" I ask, a challenge for him to say what he means.

"Die."

The fire pops nearby and the hurricane outside is as loud as ever, but that word leaves a gaping silence between us. There's anguish in his furrowed eyebrows and sorrow in his downturned lips. He pulls me back in and holds me tight, and I let myself be comforted for a minute before squiggling out of his grip.

"I'm not dying."

Logan sighs the longest sigh I've ever heard. "It doesn't seem like you're doing much to stay alive."

I have nothing to say to that. He's not wrong. It's a

deeper kind of betrayal than his and Camille's. One could argue their actions prove they're living life to the fullest, while mine have shown I'm barely living, wasting all the chances Gemma will never have.

"It's not just Gemma either," he says. "Think about your parents, and Emberly, and your friends. You know, Jasmine and Cam—"

"Don't," I cut him off. "I don't want to talk about them."

"Fine." He holds his hands up in a placating way. "Think of me then. I couldn't bear losing you. You're the closest living thing to Gemma."

I open my mouth to tell him we're not the same, but he says it for me. "I know you two were very different in a lot of ways, swimming obviously." I can't help but laugh about that, which comes out all raspy and stings my throat. "But you two really did have that whole twin-not-twin thing going on."

I give him an incredulous look. Gemma and I used to joke about the twin thing, but I never really thought we were that much alike.

"There!" Logan says. "That look, right there. Gemma used to give me that look all the time when she didn't believe me. She gave it to me the first time I said I loved her. I need you around because I want to remember all those things about Gemma, and you help me do that."

He takes my hands, his eyebrows furrowed in earnestness. "There are so many reasons for you to stick around, Delta. None of us want to lose you."

"I'm doing my best." That is the truth, even if my best is not very good.

He rests his forehead against mine. His touch is different than what I feel with Emberly, no heat but still love. It's our mutual love for Gemma that passes between us.

The wind howls and thunder rumbles, and I shiver. Logan startles away from me. He reaches down and begins to take off his shirt—a black one with the name and pink logo of Gemma's favorite band—his stomach showing a little as he raises his arms.

"Stop!" I say, worried I gave him the wrong impression, that he mistook our moment for something it wasn't. "What are you doing?"

"You're soaked." He pulls off the shirt and thankfully he's wearing a plain white one underneath. "You can change into this."

"Thanks," I mumble, my cheeks warm, as I take the shirt and stand. I'm a little unsteady on my feet, but I tell Logan that I need to be alone.

"You're not gonna disappear on me?"

"Not tonight." I shrug. "Where would I go?"

The hurricane has effectively trapped us all—friends and lovers, ex-friends and ex-lovers—in this house.

Chapter 33

It's hard to stay mad at Logan, or question his love for Gemma, when he's trying hard to take care of me for her sake. It's hard *not* to question thinking he could have purposefully hurt Gemma or that he would keep it a secret if he knew someone had hurt her. Does that mean I was wrong about Camille, too, and she didn't poison Gemma? Was my sister's death a freak tragedy and I've been making things up in my head all this time? I'm not sure which thought is the worst.

I find a bathroom on the second floor. It's dark, except for when lightning strikes, which is happening more and more frequently. There's a constant rattling of the lodge from the hurricane winds.

I stare out the window. The rain has let up since I was trying to get to Emberly's car. It leaves room for me to hear the waves battering up against the shore louder than ever. A flash of lightning illuminates a giant wave, the white peak hitting a few feet from the front door, way closer than it normally gets at high tide. It's big enough to send spray shooting up the side of the lodge. So that's what the meteorologist meant when she was talking about storm surge.

I shiver again. I'm still soaking wet, and this damp house isn't helping. I peel off my shirt and bra and relish in the warmth of Logan's too-big shirt, cologne smell and all. There's not much I can do about my soaked bottom half except rub the wetness off my bare legs. My socks are soaked as well and the bandages on my feet are too wet to be salvageable. I take them off and slip my boots on over my bare feet. It's uncomfortable where the cushioned insoles squish against the bottom of my feet, and the rubber sides chafe against my calves, but there's no way I'm walking barefoot through this house.

My throat is sore and my body is achy, and I really want another beer since it seems I'm stuck here, but I have to pee. I wonder if the plumbing works, and if anyone thought to check that before deciding to throw a party here. The water is yellow in the toilet but not as bad as I was expecting, but I hover above the seat anyway, swaying a bit in my drunken state. I don't bother flushing when I'm done, not wanting to deal with what might happen.

I use my phone, which thankfully is still working despite my earlier dunking, to illuminate the hallway. Voices from the room across the hall catch my attention, and I creep up next to the door, which is cracked open a few inches.

"I don't know what to do. She seemed okay at the end of the summer, but her behavior has been so erratic since school started." I recognize Emberly's voice, but it sounds breathy and upset. I scoot a little closer to the door to hear better over the noise of the storm. "She mostly seems okay when we're together. But then she says weird things about what she does when she's alone. Like today when I got to her house, her feet were all cut up. She said she went out for a run and put her sweaty feet in the water to cool off and stepped on shells. That doesn't sound like something she would do. It's hard to believe her." She makes a strangled sobbing noise. "And I'm still not sure what she was doing when Logan found her. I thought bringing her here tonight would be good, that maybe she'd make up with you two, but it's just been a disaster."

I don't dare to peek into the room, even with it being so dark, but I assume Emberly is talking to Jasmine and Camille. I can't believe the three of them are in there talking about me. My heart beats fast just thinking about it; the storm inside me churning up again.

Here I was feeling bad about accusing Camille of poisoning Gemma. I remind myself, poison or not, she still betrayed Gemma by hooking up with Logan. The anger takes the sting out hearing Emberly's loud sobs. It brings a pang of regret, but it's not all on me. If Emberly thought bringing me to this party would mean making up with them —especially Camille—then she's partly to blame for her sorrow.

"Hey, okay, okay," comes Jasmine's voice.

"What she said tonight about Camille poisoning Gemma, it makes me so worried." With that statement, Emberly manages, in between hiccups and sobs, to send another dagger right into my back. "I don't think it's just grief anymore. She sounds paranoid. And I don't know how to help her."

My heart is in my throat as I listen to my girlfriend, the one person who has consistently been there for me since Gemma died, basically admit she thinks I'm delusional.

"I'm not sure you can help her," Camille says, confirming she's in on this bash Delta fest.

"Her parents get home next week, right?" says Jasmine. "I think one of us needs to talk to them about it. Until then, we do what we have to to keep her safe."

"Oh shit!" Emberly says, and my heart is in my throat, thinking something bad has happened to her. "I lost my bracelet."

"We'll help you look for it," says Camille.

Now that I know it's just Emberly's stupid bracelet

gone missing, I'm done being worried and back to being furious. One part of me wants to storm in there and really let loose on them. The other part wants to run back into the hurricane and dive into those choppy waters. My heart pounds hard in my chest, but it's nothing compared to my inner storm, not one of grief this time but rage.

They think they need to save me, but the person who needed saving was Gemma. She was the one in danger, and it's too late to save her so they've turned on me. This act of being my savior makes me think they all have a guilty conscious. Even if they didn't do something to hurt Gemma, maybe they knew something that could have helped her but didn't say anything. Something Gemma took at the party, but they did it too and were too cowardly to risk getting in trouble.

Maybe not Emberly, she came into the picture later and is probably just buying into what everyone else is saying. But certainly Camille, Logan, and Jasmine could know something that might have saved Gemma.

Who knows? Emberly could be in on it, too. She was at that last party before Gemma got sick. I think back to that night. I wasn't wasted, but my memories have that party haze around them. I was with Emberly most of the night, but there could've been a moment when we weren't together. I rub my temples, a headache mounting, and try to remember. What did I miss that night?

I'm so lost in thought, I almost don't hear the shuffle of movement as the three of them head to the door. Just in time to avoid getting caught eavesdropping, I slip back into the bathroom across the hall.

"Maybe it fell off upstairs while we were dancing..." Jasmine trails off as they move down the hall.

With my back up against the wall, my rapid heartbeat

reverberating loudly, I strain to hear footsteps heading up the stairs to the third floor. All the while, the house shudders under the battering of the hurricane, grumbling and rattling like it knows all of us in here are rotten and it would love nothing better than expel us into the elements.

I shake along with the Sea Glass Lodge. Bile rises in my throat, and I get sick into the toilet that's getting nastier by the minute. I rest my head against the cool wall, but it does nothing to temper my turmoil.

All my friends betrayed me, and I'm stuck in this decrepit lodge with them.

Beware the storm.

Gemma was right all along.

Chapter 34

Intending to drink myself into oblivion until I can get out of this house, I go back to the party floor. The disco ball is spinning, but the music is no longer playing. I check my phone and see cell service is out, so our phones are basically glorified flashlights at this point. The kegs work, though, and that's what I came for.

The party has settled into smaller pockets of people. A group of juniors plays cards in one spot, while the seniors have gathered in another chatting and laughing. A couple leans up against one of the small wall spaces between the windows, making out, their bodies entwined so I can't tell where one person ends and the other begins.

Emberly, Jasmine, and Camille sit close together near the spiral staircase up to the crow's nest. Their shoulders are hunched conspiratorially as if they've brought their bash Delta party up here. When Emberly glances up and spots me, she quickly comes over. I step behind the keg to keep space between us.

"Delta!" she says. "You're still here."

"The road is flooded." I shrug like the rushing waters didn't almost take me down for good. "Logan didn't tell you?"

"I haven't seen him since you left." She rubs her hands together. Nervously or guiltily? It's hard to tell with so many secrets and lies between us.

I briefly wonder where Logan went after his knight in shining armor bit, but I have other things to worry about right now. Mainly getting drunk.

I take the key fob out of my soggy pocket and toss it to Emberly. "Sorry, I dropped it in the water."

"Oh." She looks down at the key fob and back up at my face, clearly confused by my cold demeanor. What did she expect? Kisses and roses? Would she even want those after my unhinged outburst?

I pour beer into my cup, my keg technique lacking compared to Parker's, so it ends up half full of foam. I down the contents in a few quick glugs and fill it up again.

"So we're stuck here?" Emberly asks. "For how long?" She checks her phone, a dismayed look pursing her lips when she undoubtedly discovers service is down.

"Until the storm blows over, I guess." I shrug and gulp down more beer. It's room temperature and not exactly refreshing. Plus, it burns as it goes down my sore throat, but with enough beer, that'll numb things up, hopefully along with my feelings. I take another drink.

"Delta, don't you think you should slow down?" Emberly says.

"What are you, my mom?" I fill the cup a third time and find it's hard to keep my hand steady, which means I'm making progress on getting ripping drunk. I giggle.

Emberly puts her smooth hand on my forearm, the one holding the beer. "Seriously. The storm's only going to get worse and who knows when we'll get out of here? I don't think it's a good idea to get too drunk."

Everyone—except Parker and Logan, who are still MIA—is watching our exchange. I turn my gaze away from Emberly and offer a dazzling smile to everyone else.

"I think it's the perfect time to be drunk. You all," I do a sweeping gesture and accidentally spill some beer. "Oops, party foul. What was I saying?" I sway a little but keep my feet under me. "Oh right. You all think I'm out of my mind and this stupid storm," I'm yelling now, my chin raised to direct my anger at the hurricane, "has trapped me here. So, yeah, it's the perfect time to be drunk."

If anyone had any confidence left in my sanity, my speech has eroded that faster than the hurricane is eroding the shoreline. I laugh away everyone's shocked faces and stagger my way to one of the south-facing windows. With the spinning lights inside, it's hard to see anything but distorted reflections. Not that I need to see how bad the storm is; it's easy enough to hear it. The wind batters the windows, and water flows in streaks across them.

It's just as well that I can't see anything outside because that means no chance of spotting Gemma. Is her ghost out there somewhere, unable to tell me the truth of what happened but also unable to find rest? A hellish purgatory, making my life hell as well.

The lodge moans under the wind like a thousand angry ghosts trying to get inside. We're in for it now. What time did that meteorologist say the eye of the hurricane would make landfall? Midnight, I think.

I glance back into the room. Emberly has joined Jasmine and Camille, their heads huddled back together, an occasional glance sent my way. The other groups have gone back to their chatting and games. The kissing couple is gone, probably to find a more private place. On a different day, that might have been me and Emberly sneaking off to be alone, but not tonight.

Logan and Parker pop up from the second floor. They're shirtless and soaking, looking like they're all oiled up for a photo shoot. A couple of the juniors whistle, but Logan shoots them a nasty look. He raises his arms, one hand holding a big, black flashlight, to get our attention, but everyone's already looking at him.

"Parker and I went to check out the conditions," he says. "Water's coming in from all sides. We barely made it back in. There's basically a river to the north, blocking us off from the cars. The Sound has reached the front of the house."

"Delta already told us we're stuck here," one of the seniors says.

Logan shoots a look my way, and I notice the heaviness of his eyes that suggests a bone-weary tiredness I'm very familiar with. "Yeah, we're definitely stuck. We should probably move to the second floor. Less windows down there. I think the wind is only going to get worse."

"Not the first floor?" Emberly asks, the uneasy waver in her voice obvious...well obvious to me anyway. My traitor heart gives a pang, and I almost go over there to comfort her.

"The front door broke." Logan shoots another look my way, which is unfair because it wasn't my fault the wind destroyed the door when I opened it. "Parker and I did our best to board it up, but if the water keeps rising, it's only a matter of time before it gets inside."

Logan's little announcement has dampened the mood of the party even more so than my speech. Everyone is looking sober and scared as they gather up the lights and candles to move to the second floor. That is not a place I want to be emotionally, so I take up residence at the kegs and drink some more. Sips now instead of gulps because my stomach is bloated and my head's spinning.

Emberly keeps shooting me looks as she picks up candles, like I'm due north in the compass of the room. I glower and settle into my spot. That keeps her from approaching me. Finally, everyone shuffles down the stairs, until only Emberly, Logan, and I are left.

Emberly takes one last hopeful look in my direction, but I turn away and watch out of the corner of my eye as she heads down the stairs.

Logan stands with his arms across his bare chest. "Come on, Delta."

I consider arguing with him. Instead, I take my time filling up my cup, and then I rush past him as fast as my inebriated state will allow.

The stairway is dark, even with Logan's flashlight shining down the stairs from behind, but I safely make my way down. The second-floor hallway is closed in and claustrophobic compared to the open third floor.

I feel more trapped than ever.

Chapter 35

Everyone's gathered in the bedroom where Emberly, Jasmine, and Camille were talking about me. A tacky brass four-poster bed is the only furniture in the room. There's no mattress or box spring, so the frame's a boxy skeleton partitioning the room.

It's a centrally-located room with a single window, and it's probably one of the safer places to ride out the storm. I wouldn't mind a better view than the pale, scared faces surrounding me. The mood so quickly changed from party fun to trapped in an old beach house during a hurricane.

I'm very drunk now, so it all seems a little hilarious. Like what did they think was going to happen when they came here tonight? We all knew the storm was coming. Of course bad things were going to happen. Joke's on them for tricking their parents into letting them come. Maybe this is Gemma's way of getting revenge. She warned me, not them.

Beware the storm.

And the worst is probably yet to come. Nothing good can come of this combination of people out here on a night like tonight.

The hurricane barrels along outside, tearing all kinds of strange noises from the house, but no one inside makes much noise. It's an awkward not-silence. The disco ball is off, so flashlights and candles provide the only light. The flickering flames give everyone an eerie, quivering glow. They're all ghosts. I stare at every face to make sure Gemma's not hidden among the living.

A damp coldness permeates the room, though my insides and face are warm from the beer. Jasmine and Camille huddle with Emberly on the floor inside the bed frame. Camille shoots me a look that says, "Don't you dare try to cross over that brass boundary."

With such a cool welcome, I perch in the doorway, not sure where to go. Logan's behind me, and I scoot to the side to let him in. I forgot he wasn't wearing a shirt. He wraps his arms around his chest, cold or uncomfortable…or both.

"You want your shirt back?" I ask him.

He shakes his head. "I'm fine."

Parker pushes their way into the room, also shirtless, but they look perfectly comfortable that way. Their hands are full of drinks, and they pass them out to try and bring back the party atmosphere. "C'mon, people! It's still a party."

They try to turn on the disco ball, but the batteries must have run out because it doesn't respond to the button being pushed repeatedly.

"I'll get more drinks," Parker declares, unfazed by the less-than-enthusiastic response.

"I'll help," I say, not wanting to be in this depressing room another minute. It's totally killing my buzz.

Emberly shoots me a worried look, but the wailing wind distracts her and I slip out unnoticed. I follow Parker to the third floor, their flashlight bobbing up and down as we climb the stairs. Parker glances back at me, face alternately pale and shadowy. Everything looks like it could be a ghost.

I stumble on the last step and fall into Parker, slipping off their wet back and falling sideways onto the floor. Parker's balance is knocked off kilter and they fall too. For some reason, this is the funniest thing to ever happen and we crack up, unable to stop laughing for several minutes. When my stomach hurts from laughing so hard, I flop on my back.

"I'd say let's bring a whole keg down, but I doubt we'd make it," I say. "I'm way too drunk for that."

Parker laughs again. "Me too. I didn't know you were such a party girl, Delta."

"Me neither." It suddenly occurs to me that I haven't seen Jasmine and Parker lip-locked once tonight. "What's going on with you and Jasmine?" I blurt out before I can stop myself.

They pause long enough to make me regret asking, but they finally say carefully, "She broke up with me. How can you not know that?"

Good question. Luckily, before I can dissect why I didn't know that my best friend broke up with her partner, Parker reaches into their pocket and produces a beat-up joint. "You want?"

"Yes." Anything to make this night better.

"It's kind of soggy, but I think it'll be alright if we can light it."

It takes a few tries, but Parker lights it up and takes a hit before handing it to me. We pass it back and forth, some of the leaves falling out where there's a small tear in the paper. It's oddly peaceful. I'm not sure if I'm getting used to the sound of the hurricane—it's kind of become soothing in a white noise kind of way—or if I'm so fucked up, I just don't have the senses to properly hear it.

"Hey!" I have another sudden thought. "Where's Briggs?" He and Parker are always together at parties.

"His parents wouldn't let him come out tonight."

I take a hit of the joint and blow out the smoke thoughtfully. "I didn't realize his parents were strict like that."

"They didn't used to be, but ever since that party at his house, they've been paying more attention to what he's been doing."

"Oh." We both know what party they're talking about—Gemma's last one. Parker mentioning it has caught me off-guard. "Did you both get questioned about Gemma?"

I avoid looking in Parker's direction, but we're close enough for me to feel them shrug. "Not me, but Briggs did. I think it freaked his parents out." Parker moves, and I feel their gaze upon me without having to look in their direction. "You know I'm really sorry about Gemma, right? You've probably heard it like a million times, but I wanted you to know."

I was ready to be mad, but they sound so sincere, I'm actually a little touched. "Thanks, Parker." For the first time maybe ever, I find I want to talk about it to someone other than Emberly. "I miss her so much, it hurts. Like there's this pain in my chest that never goes away and sometimes it hurts so bad, I can't breathe."

Parker passes me the joint, and I sneak a peek at them to see they're looking up at the ceiling. "Grief fucks you up." They say it like they know the truth of it. "My nana died when I was thirteen. We were really close...she had kind of raised me up until then. I was so messed up about it, I got into all kinds of trouble. Just stupid shit because I didn't know what to do with all the pain."

"Yeah" is all I say. What else is there to say? If you know that feeling, you know nothing makes it better. Not the stupid declarations of "I'm sorry" or the donations or the flowers. None of it. "Does it still hurt like when it first happened?"

"Nah," they say, sure of the answer. "It sucks still, but

the hurt...it doesn't go away, but it kind of...fades into something that lets you breathe again."

We are back to talking without looking at one another, both lost in our own fields of vision. But then I sense Parker glance at me, and I meet their gaze. Parker takes the last hit of the joint, keeping eye contact with me the whole time, even as they blow smoke out of their mouth and it swirls up all around us. For a moment, Parker sees me—really sees me in a way I'd never expect from them.

Then they cross their eyes, smash the roach of the joint on the ground, and make a farting sound on their forearm. We crack up again.

It's at that moment that a huge gust of wind makes a noise like a freight train. Somehow I feel the way it swoops around the house, my ears popping from the pressure. The trapdoor at the top of the spiral staircase flaps once, twice, and then blows clear off.

As water rushes in and cascades down the metal stairs, a numbness overtakes me, sweet relief from all the pain. And inside of me, a reckless energy rises, fed by the chaos of the storm.

Chapter 36

"Well, shit," Parker says, while watching water spill into the room. "Let's bring the alcohol down and see if we can find something to board that up."

We gather up as many bottles and mixers as we can and go back to the damp, depressing room on the second floor.

The energy that infused me the moment the trapdoor blew off wraps around me like a protective blanket. I'm not scared of the storm or what my friends think or even of seeing Gemma's ghost.

Being trapped in the Sea Glass Lodge where almost everyone is scared has given me an epiphany. My sister dying was one of the worst things that could have happened. When the worst thing happens, there's really nothing left to be scared of.

Sure, my mom or stepdad could die, too. That would be another worst thing. But worrying about it isn't going to keep it from happening. There was nothing I could have done to prevent Gemma's death, whether a medical mystery or murder by poisoning. Obviously, the doctors couldn't save Gemma, so what could I—a regular person—have done? And if it was poison, there was no earthly reason for me to suspect Camille, so again, nothing I could have done.

Bad shit, like worst-case scenario stuff, happens all the time. And there's nothing any of us can do to stop it. So what's the point of all the worry? Fuck the worry...fuck the panic attacks.

If something bad happens tonight, the time to have prevented it is long past. We're all here now and there's nothing we can do about it, so I'm not going to waste any more time worrying about it. I wasted my whole damn summer; I'm done with that.

I put the drinks on the floor for whoever might want them and march up to Logan. "The storm blew the trapdoor off upstairs. Is there anything in the house to board it up?"

"What happened?" Cassie, one of the seniors from the swim team, asks in a panicked voice.

"The trapdoor blew off and water's getting in." My words are clipped with impatience.

"How much water?" she asks.

I roll my eyes. "Enough. Logan? Anything?"

"Yeah," he says. "I think we can find something downstairs."

Emberly hops over the brass bed frame and intercepts me as I head for the door. "What's going on?"

Her big brown eyes are wide with so much worry. I want to hug her and tell her it will be okay. And if it's not going to be okay, then I'd tell her there's nothing we can do about it. But I'm still mad at her.

"Nothing. There's just something we need to take care of upstairs."

She takes my hand in her gentle way, and I let her because I love her, despite all that's happened tonight. "I'm sorry I made you come here. We never should have left your house."

For some reason, I find that funny. My laugh starts out harsh but eventually turns real, until I'm doubled over, clutching my stomach. I blame the reaction on the pot; Parker always has the strongest stuff.

When I recover, I straighten up to find Emberly biting

her bottom lip.

"What's going on with you?" she asks. "Are you high?"

"Very." I glance at Parker, who shoots me a guilty smile. And it makes me laugh again, but not quite as hard.

Lightning flashes bright enough to illuminate the whole room through the one window. It highlights Emberly's stricken face, and I feel sorry for her. She's stuck in that place I was stuck in all summer: the worry spiral.

So I hug her and say, "It's gonna be okay."

And I leave her with that statement. For real, though, what the hell do I know? Nothing's felt alright for a long time, but maybe it's starting to now. Either way, I've got a job to do.

Logan, Parker, and I head downstairs, Logan leading the way with a flashlight. The noise of the storm is different here, lower-pitched with a steadier rhythm. It's the difference between the wind and the waves, as the crash of water on the house drowns out the sound of the wind.

We check on the front door where Logan and Parker patched it up. The churning water outside echoes in the hallway. Parker stares longingly at the last untapped keg, and I shake my head in a way that says "no way we're getting that thing upstairs right now."

Logan presses on the boards nailed to the broken door. "It's holding up so far," he says with satisfaction. "C'mon to the kitchen. That's where we found the wood."

A hammer and nails are scattered across a countertop that runs the length of one side of the kitchen. There are empty spaces where an oven and fridge should be. They remind me of the spaces Gemma has left behind. I feel them now, no longer filled with grief. The storm inside me has quieted, and maybe that's me healing. Maybe I need to feel the emptiness in order to heal. Not move on, that's not the right phrase for it, more like finding a new normal. One without my sister, my best friend, my twin-not-twin.

The thought makes me sigh long and low, and Logan shoots me a sideways glance. He disappears into a big pantry, which was probably once filled with food staples like flour and spices, but is mostly empty now, a lone mop propped up in the corner.

"We used shelves for the front door," Logan says, "but there's none left."

"What about the cabinet doors?" I suggest.

"That's a great idea." Logan spins around, the light from the flashlight bobbing around like crazy.

The motion does something weird to my equilibrium. Black spots dance in my vision, and the floor feels like it moves out from underneath my feet.

Gemma's face appears above me. Gemma's ghostly face.

"Delta." Her face is twisted in agony. "I told you 'beware the ssstorm.' Why didn't you listen?"

I try to reach out to touch her cheek but find I'm unable to move my arms. So I smile. "It's okay. I figured it out. If something bad is going to happen, it's out of my control. I shouldn't worry about it anymore. You can rest now. I'll be okay, and if I'm not, you're dead, so you can't do anything about it."

Gemma's mouth has a stubborn twist to it, the one she used to give me when she disagreed with me but knew I wouldn't listen. "But you had control of whether or not you came here. You shouldn't have come here, not in the ssstorm."

I'm not sure how much control I did have over coming here; fate seems to have led me here despite my attempts to thwart it. "But I'm here. And I can't change that, so it's time to move on. You have to move on, Gemma. Find wherever it is you're supposed to be."

"I can't." She looks so sad, and scared.

"You can. You have to. You can't keep haunting me."

"No." She looks left and right, her head flitting in and out of transparency as she moves. "You don't undersssstand. I can't leave here. I—" Her speech cuts off and her mouth opens in that awful silent scream.

I try to reach for her, but my arms won't budge. "Gemma!" She flicks out of view and back in. "Gemma!"

Her image flickers out one last time, and then all I see is black.

Chapter 37

I wake up to Logan shouting my name. Nausea wraps itself around my stomach when I take Logan's hand to help me sit. I'm going to be sick. I rush to the kitchen sink just in time. Logan graciously holds back my hair as I empty my stomach. He turns on the tap, and brownish water washes down the worst of it. When I'm done, I slide to the floor.

Parker hands me a stick of gum. "I think that's partly my fault. I forgot you don't usually smoke."

"There's not even clean water to give you," Logan says. "We should've canceled this party. It was a bad idea to have it in the storm." He shivers.

I remember the jackets Emberly and I left in the living room and send Parker to get them. There's no need for Parker and Logan to be running around the lodge half-naked. Plus, I want to talk to Logan alone. I have to settle this thing between me, Logan, and Camille.

Logan runs his hand through his hair and leaves it sticking up funny. "What the hell were we thinking?"

"I don't think any of us have been thinking clearly," I say. "Logan, you swear on your mother's life that Camille had nothing to do with Gemma's death."

"Yes, Delta!" Logan throws his hands up. "I swear on everything. I swear on—"

"Don't say Gemma's grave," I interrupt. "I believe you." That is the truth. I'm finally realizing how wrong it was to think Camille would hurt Gemma. No one knows what caused Gemma to get sick—and we may never know—but I no longer think someone poisoned Gemma.

Besides," I crack a smile through chapped lips, "she doesn't have a grave." Her ashes in that black box are depressing as hell, but it's my mom's job to decide what to do with them, and she deserves as much time as she needs for that.

Logan leans his head back against the cabinets under the sink. "I hate that she's not here. I miss talking to her the most. She was such a good listener."

"She was," I say so quietly, my heart in my throat, that I'm not sure he hears me over the crashing waves and the howling wind.

I look at him to find tears streaking down his face. He sort of collapses in on himself and sobs into his knees. Parker's back and they wrap a jacket around Logan. I enfold him in my arms. My throat is tight and my chest is tight, but there are no tears for me. Sitting here on this dirty kitchen floor comforting Logan, my heart hurts for him and what he lost, which leaves a little less room for my own pain. Parker sits on the other side of Logan, a silent witness to our mourning.

I'm not sure how long we stay like that, Logan's shoulders shaking under my embrace, the moaning of the wind a proper backdrop for the pain of loss. Lightning strikes and thunder crashes, but we're in our own bubble, impervious to what's going on outside.

When he's ready, Logan sits up and wipes his face. He smiles, sadness still in his eyes, and pats my arm. That's when I finally let go of him. A persistent ache is heavy in my chest, but the storm of grief stays under control. It's not churning as it once did, or maybe I've grown stronger around it.

"Shit," Logan says. "Sorry about that. I feel like I should be comforting you, not the other way around. I loved

Gemma, but not like you did."

"No, it's good to be on the other side." Perhaps always being the one crying and never the shoulder to cry on isn't healthy. Just like it's not healthy to always be the shoulder. Like Emberly has been for me all summer. And when she spent one morning being vulnerable—in an attempt to help me—I was a crap shoulder for her.

Logan stretches his arms and cracks his knuckles. "Alright, let's take apart these cupboards before everyone upstairs is treading water."

We get to work on the biggest ones, which will cover the largest area with less work. My legs are wobbly, but I don't feel like passing out or throwing up. There were no screwdrivers where Logan and Parker found the hammer and nails, so we do our best with the claw part of the hammer to pull the screws out without destroying the wood.

It's high-quality wood, too. It makes me wonder what this place looked like when it was new. Probably gorgeous. The floor in the kitchen is a nice hardwood, in need of a few patches in places, but overall in good shape considering the abandoned state of the property and the beating it must take from the salty air. I wonder if there's hardwood under the moldy carpet in the rest of the house.

We manage to get off one cupboard intact, so we get to work on a second. Now that I'm thinking about the Sea Glass Lodge, scrutinizing what I've seen of it, the state of it doesn't make sense. There isn't a single broken window, which is unusual for a vacant house that high schoolers use for parties. The work of art that is the sea-glass window makes me think someone once loved it as a home. I figure someone must come by on occasion and take care of it.

And now we're destroying their kitchen. But it's a necessary evil in a desperate time.

My head spins a little as we fully separate the second cupboard from the shelves. I've had a lot to drink tonight, and none of it water, unless you count the water I inhaled when I fell outside. And I've smoked two joints. Honestly, I'm not sure how I'm still standing.

I lean against the counter and swallow, the nausea rising once more. Not that there's anything left in my stomach to expel, but that won't keep me from dry heaving. The thought fills my mouth with saliva. All the blood rushes from my head, and I think I might pass out again, so I sit on the floor.

Logan and Parker cease their grunting over a third—and by our calculations final—cupboard when they notice me. I wave them away because I don't want them to fuss over me, but they come over anyway.

"You okay?" Logan asks. "You're really pale."

I must look really bad for him to be able to tell that with only one flashlight propped up to light the room.

"I'm still pretty drunk and high," I say, though my thoughts have been surprisingly clear and insightful since I smoked that second joint with Parker.

"We're idiots for not having water," says Logan.

"Don't look at me." Parker puts their hands up in a declaration of innocence. "I was in charge of the alcohol, and we've got plenty of that."

"We've all been idiots." The wave of dizziness passes, and I stand. "I'm alright. Let's get this last cupboard and repair that trapdoor."

After a few more minutes of clawing with the hammer and pulling on the cupboard, it comes loose. The three of us let out a cheer of triumph as we set it down on top of the other two.

Our victory is short-lived when we hear a high-pitched scream from upstairs, followed by shouting. My heart pounds, but my breathing remains steady. One quick look between the three of us and we bolt to the staircase. Cassie meets us at the bottom.

"What happened?" Logan asks.

Cassie holds up a hand to give herself a moment to catch her breath. "She's headed for the roof. Camille and Jasmine went after her, yelled for me to come and get you." She points at me.

"Emberly," I whisper. It has to be her. My instinct is to push past everyone and charge up the stairs, but panic rises in me and I clutch my chest.

Not now, I think. I've got to be there for Emberly.

Logan grabs my shoulders. "You okay, Delta?"

I picture Emberly telling me to "breathe" in that calming way she has. It's my turn to be there for her, like I was there for Logan earlier. The thought of being strong for someone else helps me get the air back into my lungs.

I turn to Cassie. "Move!"

I'm coming, Emberly.

Chapter 38

Anxiety seizes me at the thought of Emberly being in trouble. It's different than what I've been feeling. The panic attacks brought on by Gemma's death are breath-stopping and paralyzing. This sense of panic charges me with adrenaline and propels me up the stairs faster than my drunk ass should be able to move.

I fly through the second-floor hallway, ignoring the curious faces peeking out at me. My legs burn as I climb the next flight of stairs, but I ignore the pain. It's purely physical; much easier to push past than the emotional pain I've been dealing with.

I reach the third floor just in time to see Emberly's legs disappear at the top of the metal spiral staircase, water still pouring down them, onto the crow's nest.

"Emberly!" Jasmine and Camille yell from the bottom. They are bowed against the water.

I charge across the room. "Move!"

They scurry out of my way, and I bound up the slippery spirals, having to slow down so as not to fall. When I reach the top, I'm hit with humid air that also somehow manages to be chilling. The wind pulls at me from all directions, sending stinging rain into my face.

I don't bother to try and clear the water from my face as I search for Emberly. It's so dark, and I wish I'd grabbed a flashlight. The noise and wind are like a helicopter trying to land on my head.

"Emberly!" I yell, but my voice gets snatched away by the elements.

I fight my way across the roof. It's hard to stay on a straight course. The wind pushes me to one side, and I brace myself against it, only to be shoved in the opposite direction. I keep my hands outstretched, hoping they brush the railing before I end up over the edge.

Lightning streaks down from the clouds, hits the choppy waters of the Sound, and illuminates the sky. I see a flash of Emberly. She stands at the railing, looking out over the water. Thunder rumbles almost the second the light is gone. At least I think it's thunder; it's hard to tell among the roaring wind and rain.

"Emberly!" I scream again.

Another flash of lightning allows me to see her face as she turns toward me. It's pale and haunted, like *she's* a ghost.

Now that I know which direction to go, I push forward as best I can while getting buffeted around by the wind. I know I've reached her when I bump into something warm.

My hands shake, my whole body shivers, as I reach for her. We are both so wet, my hands slip right off her arms as I try to hold her. I can't see her very well in this blinding rain and dark, but her warmth confirms she's not a ghost. I find her hand in the dark, a cold contrast to the rest of her.

A great gust of wind blows me off my feet, thankfully backward onto the roof and not over the edge. I keep hold of Emberly's hand, and she falls on top of me. I've never been so thankful in all my life that the wind sent us this way and not into the depths of the water. I grab her, wrapping my arms and legs around her. She fights the embrace, but I hold firm.

As we struggle on the roof, a thought rings clear above the tumult of the hurricane: I have to control the storm of grief inside me before it destroys everything I hold dear.

It's at that moment the rain and wind abruptly stop. The sudden change is almost as disorientating as the force of the hurricane. It takes me a minute to realize what's going on.

The eye of the storm.

"Emberly," I say now that she might actually hear me. "Stop fighting me."

She does the exact opposite and kicks me in the stomach, the pain exploding through my body and stopping my breath. My arms fall limp and I involuntarily let go of her.

As if by magic, moonlight reaches us from the break in the clouds. Emberly stands over me, her eyes glassy and unfocused. She rushes to the edge of the roof. Still not quite able to catch my breath, I scramble up and pump my legs. My boots search for purchase on the soaked surface, and it's a miracle I find it.

Emberly has one leg over the edge of the railing in the same damn spot I climbed over the other day. There's no dead sister haunting her, but maybe there are other ghosts urging her on—the ghosts we all have inside of us, born from doubt and pain.

I surge to the railing as she gets her second leg over. She holds her arms out to the side, ready to fly...ready to fall!

In an act of bravery or madness—or both—and certainly in an act of love, I slam into the railing, not sparing a thought for the fact that it might not hold me. I reach my arms out as far as I can. My fingers brush against Emberly's back, clutch at her shirt.

With strength I didn't know I possessed, I squeeze the

fabric in my fist and hold fast. The full weight of her body pulls at me. The railing digs into my flesh. I try and wrap my other arm around her waist, my hold tenuous, desperate. I grip her shirt tighter, my hand cramping. As my strength begins to fail, I will her to stay on this roof. If the wind had still been blowing, we surely would've already fallen to the churning waters crashing against the house.

I reach a tipping point, let go or go over with her. I don't let go. I won't let go.

A force from behind pulls me back, away from the railing. The sudden lessening of weight almost causes me to let go of Emberly. My cramping hand has nearly lost all feeling, but somehow I don't let go. Once Emberly's back is up against the railing, a second set of hands lifts her over and onto the safe side of the crow's nest. We all fall down... for me, out of sheer exhaustion.

In a beam of moonlight that reaches out from the patch of open sky above, I see three faces. Jasmine's stricken one, her arms clutched around Emberly like she'll never let go. Camille's wan with relief, her body close beside me. Then there's Emberly. She looks confused at first, like she doesn't know what she's doing up here on the crow's nest. Her eyes widen in fear, like she suddenly remembers what she's doing up here.

I crawl the short way to her and practically tackle her. The need to touch her, to prove that she's flesh and blood and intact, overcomes me.

I bury my face in her chest and sob. We're both shaking. Warm arms wrap around us, and I'm happy to have my friends here. Friends that are here despite my awful behavior. We'll only ever be three-quarters of the inseparable foursome, but it's better than being alone.

And now we have Emberly. My sobs renew in fervor

as my brain replays how close I came to losing her.

"I'm…" Emberly begins, and I unbury my face to see her looking around at us. "I'm sorry. I—"

Now it's my turn to hold her against *my* chest and let her sob. The moon passes behind the clouds and it gets darker, and colder.

"We should get back inside," Camille says in a hoarse voice. She must have been yelling before, but I never heard anything. All my focus had been on holding onto Emberly. My legs are wobbly like jelly as we head to the opening to the stairs. I keep my arm around Emberly, never wanting to let go of her again.

I can't believe my selfishness almost sent her over the edge.

Supporting Emberly down the stairs, I silently vow to be better at emotionally supporting my girlfriend. In order to do that, I realize I need to be in a better place myself.

I glance at Jasmine and Camille; I also need to work on being a better friend.

Chapter 39

Logan and Parker get to work boarding up the trapdoor while the skies are momentarily clear. The timing of the eye of the hurricane is fortuitous in more ways than one. I have no idea how things would have gone down if we hadn't had a lull in the storm to save Emberly.

Everyone else stares with haunted eyes when we get back into the room on the second floor. Cassie looks at us quizzically, and I subtly shake my head to indicate not to ask about what happened. She nods in understanding and brings up another topic.

"It got so quiet. We thought maybe the hurricane had passed."

"It's the eye of the storm."

Cassie's eyes grow big and white against her tan face. "So it's only half over? It was a bad idea to come here tonight."

I shrug; it's a revelation I think we've all had about this place and this night. "Yeah."

The quiet is unnerving, and I almost wish the eye would pass already. Emberly rests her head on my shoulder where we sit propped up against the wall. Jasmine and Camille settle nearby, shooting furtive glances at Emberly. She hasn't said anything since the roof, and with a drawn expression and bags under her eyes, she appears utterly exhausted. She looks how I feel, tired to the bone. Nearly losing Emberly has sobered me up, and I won't drink or smoke anymore tonight. I've had enough of trying to bury my feelings.

Emberly's been shivering since we left the crow's nest, and it's becoming more pronounced the longer we sit. I think maybe she's in shock. I look around, not sure what I'm searching for to help, when I spot the drink mixers and juice Parker and I brought down earlier.

"Can you get the cranberry juice?" I ask Jasmine.

When she hands me the bottle, I don't bother with a cup, instead unscrewing the cap and holding it up to Emberly's lips. "Drink."

She looks at me with surprise, like she hasn't been aware of her surroundings. At least she does what I tell her and takes a few sips. Yet the shivering continues.

I turn to Jasmine and Camille. "What do we do?"

Giving Emberly juice was my only idea. My brain is sluggish, and my body feels heavy with achiness. My breathing has turned a little labored again, though it's not accompanied by the signature tightness in my chest that usually marks rising anxiety.

"There's the fire," Camille suggests. We seem to have come to an unspoken truce for the moment, but I know we'll have to talk soon. I, for one, need to apologize, but there are some things I'd like her to answer for also.

"Let me check what it's like down there first." Who knows if the boarded-up door is intact against the surging tide and waves?

I press a kiss to Emberly's temple. "I'll be right back." She stares at me listlessly, and Jasmine takes my place as her pillow.

A pang goes through my heart at the thought of letting Emberly out of my sight, but I doubt she has the energy to go anywhere. And I hope her mind is in a better state than it was up on the crow's nest. She really did look horrified when she realized what she had almost done as if she had been in a trance before that and had no control over what was happening.

I grab a flashlight and head for the hallway. I pass Parker and Logan on the way.

"Is Emberly okay?" Logan asks.

"I don't know," I answer honestly. "She can't seem to stop shivering, so I'm going to see if it's safe to sit by the fire."

Logan gives Parker a look that I can't interpret. "I'll go with you." He holds up the hammer. "See if I need to add more boards to the door."

We're in the downstairs hallway, Logan hovering as I head into the room with the fireplace, when I realize why he followed me. I swing around and catch him staring, a guilty expression on his face.

"I know what you're doing." I clear my throat, a tickling sensation in my chest, probably from all the shouting up on the roof. "You don't have to watch over me."

"I'm not," he says, but I'm not buying it. "The front door looks okay, and I thought I'd help put more logs on the fire." He gestures to the hearth where the fire has burned down to embers.

Logs are stacked up next to the fireplace. Not that I need the help, but Logan insists on continuing this charade and places two logs on top of the ones I lay down.

"I'm serious, though." For some reason, I feel the need to explain myself to Logan. Maybe because of the way he found me on the beach that night or maybe because of what he said about Gemma never forgiving him if something happened to me. "I'm not going to hurt myself."

"I want to believe you, Delta." He stares at the fire as the flames come back to life. "You've just been acting so strange lately."

"I know." I cough, the tickle getting worse. Must be the smoke from the fire bothering me. "I've been in a bad place. But I'm not anymore, I promise." I hesitate, not wanting to air out Emberly's dirty laundry, but decide to gently touch on it. "Now that I've seen it from the other side, what taking your life can do to the people who love you, I realize that's not something I ever want to do to my parents or anyone. Gemma doesn't get to live, so I'm going to go out and live all the more for her."

Logan shakes his head. I'm not sure he's convinced, but I'll have to earn his trust. As he'll have to earn mine because I still don't understand how he could've hooked up with Camille so soon after Gemma's death.

Wind shakes the lodge and a gust shoots down the chimney, making the revived flames dance around madly. We must be on the other side of the eye of the hurricane. I cough again, longer than last time, this one making my eyes water.

"I should go get Emberly." The words come out wheezy. I cough and can't stop this time.

There's not enough air in the room. Or there is, but I can't get it into my lungs. I double over and continue coughing, spots floating in my vision. Logan's hand pats my back; it's so heavy on my body, I think it might push me down.

The pain and pressure in my chest are like an anxiety attack times one hundred. The storm of grief may have subsided and I may have stopped contemplating my own death, but it seems that death has a taste of me and it wants to take me for good.

I cough and cough and cough. Logan smacks my back, and I fall to the floor.

I think I might have finally figured out a way to live

in a world that doesn't include my sister, where I want to remember how to live and breathe. And now my body won't let me do those things.

Chapter 40

In a heap on the floor with my vision blurring, I cough and gasp for breath. My gasps are so loud in my head that it drowns out the sounds of the hurricane.

Logan yells for help. Soon, there's a flurry of activity around me. It all has a hazy feel to it, like I'm in a thick fog. Someone guides me to the couch and props me up in the corner.

In between coughing fits, I hear Jasmine ask, "What happened?"

"I don't know." Logan sounds far away. "She just started coughing and hasn't stopped."

"Maybe it's the smoke," says Jasmine. "Open a window."

There's a loud screech of a window being forced open, and it's like we invited the hurricane inside. Now the wind and rain are loud enough for me to hear over my wheezes and coughs. Panic rises in me, which only makes it more difficult to breathe, which makes more panic. It's a vicious feedback cycle that's trying to kill me.

"It could be a panic attack," says Emberly. "She's been having those."

Just hearing her voice calms me. Her being here, contemplating what is wrong with me, means she's feeling better. I try and find her, but my vision remains blurry and my hearing is muffled. It's hard to keep track of what's going on around me or to focus on anything except taking my next breath. My cough slowly becomes more intermittent, though it now feels like a vice is squeezing my chest.

Then Emberly is there, reaching for my hand, her cold one squeezing my warm one. I try to speak, to ask her how she's doing, but there's not enough air for that.

"Shhh," she says. "Just try to relax and breathe. Deep breath in, and deep breath out. Remember?"

Her soothing words, so familiar, bring back a million moments from this summer, until one particular evening settles in my mind. Us holding hands while we walked out as far as we could on a sandbar at low tide, the horizon so close, like standing on the edge of the world. My head resting on Emberly's shoulder while we watched the sun set behind the Sound. Emberly smelling like suntan lotion and salt water, and only a little bit like chlorine. The sky turning yellow, then bright pink, before fading to blue. The tide coming in around us, and we waited until the water lapped up our legs to head back to shore. The storm of grief set aside by awe over the beauty in front of me, next to me. Emberly.

The vice tightens around my chest, but the cough subsides enough for my vision to clear and my ears to pick up on the conversation going on around me.

"Do people cough with panic attacks?" Jasmine is practically yelling to be heard over the hurricane.

"Delta never has," Emberly says loudly. "This feels different."

"Maybe she inhaled water up on the roof?" Jasmine suggests. "Is it possible to do that from rain?"

"You think she's dry drowning?" Emberly stands, and I want her back close to me, but I can't get enough air to talk.

"What's dry drowning?" Logan asks from somewhere behind the couch where I can't see him.

A hurried discussion ensues, but my cough has returned and it's harder than ever to pay attention to their words. Stars spot my vision, a blackness creeping in around the edges.

Logan's face appears in front of mine, and he takes my hands, which have turned cold. "Oh shit, I think she is dry drowning. Earlier when she tried to leave, she fell in the water. I thought she coughed it all up."

"And you didn't think to tell us!" Camille yells.

"Her lips are turning blue." The note of panic in Emberly's voice makes my panic worse. My stomach muscles tighten painfully as I wheeze harder than ever. "We need to call 911!"

Jasmine taps her phone screen. "There's no service!"

"Just try!" Emberly is close to me, having taken Logan's place.

"I think it's going through." Jasmine proceeds to talk on her phone in the background.

My world is narrowed to the squeezing pain in my chest and Emberly's face. She tilts my chin up, her brow wrinkled in worry but a smile on her lips. "I'm going to tell you a story, and I want you to breathe nice and slow. That's all you have to do is breathe, okay?"

I manage to nod.

In her calmest voice, Emberly says, "There once was a girl who knew what it was like to be sad. The kind of sadness that fills your soul and shrouds the world in darkness, hopelessness. So she tried to end the sadness, but she failed."

Her eyes glisten with tears, but the smile stays on her lips. She keeps telling her story, and I keep breathing. "And it was a good thing she failed. A blessing. Because once she realized the sadness wasn't her fault, she saw there was light everywhere. So now when the sadness sets in, she finds the slivers of light within the dark. She knows those slivers will carry her through, and that a sliver is better than permanent darkness."

"They're gonna try and send help," Jasmine interrupts.

"Good," Emberly says in her regular voice. "You hear that, Delta. Help is coming."

Then she goes back into her story-telling voice. "One day the sad girl met another girl, and she saw that same sadness in her. Since she knew how to spot the light within the dark, she was able to see the light in her new friend. And there was so much light trying to shine through the darkness.

"The more time the two girls spent together, the more light they made. There was still sadness, particularly for the friend, who was facing hard times. But they were brave together and found the slivers of light. And they found love, the brightest light of all."

Emberly's voice is bewitching; my coughs have quieted, my breathing a little steadier, as I focus on her story—our story.

"One day a storm came." The timber of her voice goes deeper and tears spill down her cheeks. "It was so very dark for both of them. They couldn't find each other or see the slivers of light. There were no silver linings, only dark edges. The girl lost her hope again. She turned to the eternal darkness and thought there was no other way. But the friend found her, for the friend's light had been lit anew. The friend beat away the darkness, and pulled the girl back into the light. But that's not the end of the story, not even close to the end."

I double over as a new coughing fit shakes my whole

body. I ride through it with the feel of Emberly's hand rubbing circles on my back until I can sit upright again. I take a breath.

Emberly puts her forehead to mine and whispers, "Don't let your light go out."

Black remains on the edges of my vision. Instead of letting the panic take me, I focus on one breath at a time. In and out. In and out. Just like Emberly has always helped me to remember. I fight to keep the light going, for Emberly, who shared her light with me. And for Gemma, whose light will always shine no matter how long she's been dead.

But most of all for myself.

Chapter 41

I kind of lose track of time for a little while after Emberly tells me her story. Quiet voices echo around the room, but it all has that hazy edge to it. The ever-present hurricane also has that faraway feel. It's hard work focusing on my breathing, even with the cough having mostly subsided. Still, I catch snatches of conversation.

"How long did they say it would be?"

"Depends on the storm. Wind speed has to be below sixty miles per hour."

"How will they get through the water?"

"I don't know."

Emberly is never far away, periodically checking in on me and rubbing my hand gently.

Soon, lights flash around the room, and for a moment, I think someone turned on the disco ball. Then my slow-moving brain realizes it's emergency lights coming in through the windows.

"They're here!" Jasmine shouts.

"Help is here, Delta," Emberly says.

I suck in a breath, grab her arm tight as she moves away. "Stay," I wheeze.

"Okay, okay," she says. "Yes, I'll stay."

Then it's suddenly noisy and busy. Doors open and people stomp down the stairs. There are calls of "what's going on?" Other voices asking questions and answering. A man I don't recognize appears in front of me. Water drips off his firefighter helmet.

"Hi, my name is Steve," he says as he checks my

pulse. "Can you tell me your name?"

I shake my head; I used up all my power of speech asking Emberly to stay.

"It's Delta," Emberly pipes in. "Her name is Delta."

"Alright, Delta," Steve says. "You're having trouble breathing?" I nod. "I'm going to put this on you," he holds up a clear mask with a small oxygen tank attached, "to help you breathe."

I nod again to let him know I understand. He straps the mask on and tucks the tank next to me on the couch. When he turns the oxygen on, it's like taking a breath for the first time after you've been underwater. My lungs fill and it clears my head, almost too much.

For the first time since I started coughing, I'm afraid for myself. I frantically search for Emberly and find her hovering nearby. I reach out to her, and her hand finds mine.

"Delta," Steve says. "There's a lot of water outside, so we have to take you on a boat to get you to the medic."

I just squeeze Emberly's hand harder, trying to communicate for her to stay with me.

"Can I come?" Emberly asks.

Steve looks like he's about to say no, so I use up all the strength I've gained from the oxygen to pull Emberly closer to me. His gaze darts around to parts of the room I can't see, and I wonder what he must think of all of us in this abandoned beach house during a hurricane.

"Fine, she can come," he relents. "But I want the rest of you to stay put until I can get another crew out here. No one goes outside, understand? And put this fire out. I don't need any carbon monoxide issues in the meantime."

There are murmurs of agreement and more voices than I anticipated. Everyone must have come down from upstairs when the firefighters arrived. Steve speaks into his radio with an update on the situation. Then he holds up the small oxygen tank. "Can you hold this?"

I nod and take it, finding it heavier than I expected, or maybe I'm just weak. I rest it on my chest and wrap my arms around it in a hug. Now that I know Emberly is coming with me, I don't feel so panicked.

Steve scoops me up and cradles me like we're newly married and he's carrying me over the threshold. I doubt this follows any kind of firefighter protocol, but there's nothing typical about this situation.

He carries me out a door at the back of the Sea Glass Lodge. It's easy to see in the flashing lights that water comes all the way over the first two stairs off the small landing. There's an inflatable emergency boat tied up to the railing.

The wind and rain whip at us, but it doesn't feel as bad as it did when I chased Emberly onto the crow's nest. Or maybe the oxygen mask is acting as a buffer. A fire engine and an ambulance are parked beyond the flow of water, just past where our cars are parked. They're submerged in flood water up to the tops of their tires.

Steve sets me down in the boat, and I lean against the side for support. Then he picks up Emberly and deposits her next to me. We cling to each other as if we're each other's life rafts. Then Steve climbs in and untethers the raft. Immediately we're jerked down the current of this temporary river. He radios in something I can't hear over the hurricane and a second rope attached to the other side of the boat pulls us toward the fire engine. Emberly and I hold on even tighter to each other.

The rain isn't so bad now, so we're only mostly soaked by the time we make it to land. A second firefighter carries me to the back of the ambulance, while Emberly follows close behind. They make her ride up front, but I don't protest so long as she gets to come along. Steve climbs in with us as the other firefighter settles me on a gurney.

"You okay, Delta?" Steve asks.

I give him a thumbs up to let him know I'm feeling better. I'm kind of hoping they'll take me home where I can shower and try to wash this awful night away. Then I remember I probably don't have power or hot water at my house.

I hear over the radio, "En route to Regional General."

My breathing hitches at that announcement. It's the closest hospital, so I should have expected that's where I'd end up, but it's the last place I want to go.

It's the hospital where Gemma died.

Act III

"What I have done that might your nature, honor, and exception roughly awake, I here proclaim was madness."

William Shakespeare
Hamlet
Act V, Scene II

Chapter 42

The doctor at the hospital informs me that I experienced inflammation of the airway as a complication of a non-fatal drowning. It plays so well into the jokes about me not being able to swim that I would've laughed right in the doctor's face, but my throat hurts too much. I'm also dehydrated, so they hook me up to an IV. Though the inflammation has gone down, they want to keep me for observation for a few hours, at the very least until the hurricane blows over.

In a no-nonsense voice, a nurse informs me that they're working on contacting my parents, Emberly's too. My mom is going to be so worried when she hears what happened, and I'm truly sorry for putting her through more worry on behalf of one of her children, but I'm exhausted and can't think too hard about that right now.

Emberly has stayed with me through it all, a quiet presence hovering in the corner of the room. Once we're alone, she climbs into bed next to me, careful not to disturb the IV lines. She whispers in my ear that I don't need to say anything because she knows it hurts to talk. Then she tells me she loves me before I feel her breathing fall steady as she falls asleep tucked in close to me.

In the quiet of the hospital room—and it's quieter than it's been all night, the hurricane no match for the sturdy building we're in—and with the lights low, it should be easy to give in to the exhaustion and sleep. Yet sleep doesn't come.

This is where Gemma died. Before when I was having trouble breathing, I was too focused on each breath to think about Gemma dying from her lungs failing, basically from not being to breathe. Now that I can take this basic life function for granted again, the intrusive thoughts creep in. Of Gemma dying. Of her ghost. Of what happens when the great gaping maw of death comes for us all. Thoughts that easily become overwhelming if I let them.

The hospital is massive and I'm in a completely different area than where Gemma was, but I can feel death here. It's a prickle under the skin, a flutter in the chest. It's the silent pause between a last breath and oblivion.

At least I can breathe. And Emberly is close by. I try forcing my eyes shut and not thinking about what it was like for Gemma to draw her last breath here.

"Did you really talk to Gemma's ghost?" Emberly asks in a quiet voice that startles me all the same.

I sigh, long and low, and keep my eyes closed because it's easier to talk about it this way. "I don't know." I pause to try and figure out how to explain it. "It felt real in the moment...as real as talking to you right now feels. But my head hasn't been in a good place, so I might have imagined it all."

Emberly gives a thoughtful little noise but doesn't follow up with any more questions.

"What happened to you tonight?" I whisper.

It's quiet for so long, I'm not sure she heard me. But then she says, "I think I blacked out because I can't remember going up to the roof or anything until we were all lying there together. You looked so scared, and that's when I realized what I must have done. I'm sorry." There's a sharp intake of breath, like she's trying not to cry, and her body shakes. "I'm not supposed to drink or smoke with the meds I'm on. Then my bracelet went missing, and I just kind of lost it, I guess."

It's only now that I realize Emberly's woven bracelet that she's always fidgeting with is more than an accessory. I'm a selfish idiot for not noticing how she uses it to comfort herself. I've been an idiot in so many ways. I'm not sure what to say or if I could say anything to help her feel better. She scared the crap out of me and I never want to see her like that ever again.

I settle on another question, a delicate one, but it might actually help me figure out how she's really doing. "Was it like that the other time? Did you not remember what happened then either?"

It's not terribly specific, but she gets what I'm saying. "No. I remember that time very clearly. I was in my room, trying to fall asleep. I was the only one home. I had been having a hard time for a while, but I'd been pushing through okay, taking it day by day. I was doing fine with my grades and swimming. Nothing was really that bad, but also nothing made me happy."

My eyes have been closed this whole time, just me taking in her words without judgment, her chin moving against my shoulder as she speaks. "I don't know why the thought popped into my head that night. But once it did, I couldn't make it go away. So I went into my parents' bathroom and found my mom's sleeping pills. I was only going to take one, you know, to try and help me sleep. But that thought was stronger than I was, and I took the whole bottle. Then I stopped remembering and woke up in the hospital...this hospital. But I remember everything before that."

I guess there are a lot of demons in this hospital...in every hospital, I suppose. It's a place where people are saved and lost, and lives are shattered or remade.

"I'm not gonna drink anymore," Emberly says with

resolve. "I know what to do with the bad thoughts now if I have them. If drinking makes it so I can't deal with them, then that's not a risk worth taking."

I let out a breath in relief, vowing never to take for granted this wonderful miracle of being able to control the air coming in and out of my body, and open my eyes. I kiss the top of Emberly's head and find one of her hands to grasp onto. I'm happy to have her close to me, her curves fitting against mine.

Her ear is right near my mouth, so I whisper, "I'll help you in whatever way I can."

"Thanks," she says and squeezes my hand.

I kiss her earlobe. "I love you."

"Love you, too."

We're quiet then. Eventually Emberly's breathing steadies and she falls asleep for real this time. I stay awake a little longer, relishing her warmth.

Tears silently fall down my cheeks. There are so many reasons to be crying. Instead of focusing on any of them, I settle into this small moment of peace with the person I love asleep next to me. The tears don't stop, but they don't feel like they're going to break me either.

Chapter 43

Emberly and I jerk awake when her parents burst into the hospital room in the early morning hours. They whisk Emberly into the hallway where I immediately hear them lecturing her on what happened last night. While the hospital staff work on getting me discharged, I have the unfortunate opportunity to speak to my parents via the trusty landline in the hospital.

The hurricane outside has blown over, but the storm in here is just getting started.

"What were you thinking, Delta?" my mom screeches through the phone. "You almost drowned to death. How dare you? After all this family has been through..." her breath hitches loud enough for me to hear through the phone. "I can't bear to think of losing—" She can't finish because she breaks into sobs.

My stomach drops, and my throat is so thick that it's hard to swallow. I did this to her. I've caused her heart to break again.

Gary murmurs indistinct words in the background before he speaks to me. "We spoke with Emberly's parents." His voice is shaky with emotion, but at least he's not crying. "They're going to take you to Camille's, and you're to stay there until we get home. We're taking the first flight home that we can find, but it'll probably be a few days. Until then, it's school when it reopens and Camille's house, and that's it. Understand?"

"Yes," I say quietly, my throat still thick.

I don't argue, though Camille's is the last place I want

to go. I know I need to sort things out with her, but the thought of doing it this morning brings a heaviness to my body, so I stretch the phone cord and sit on the edge of the hospital bed. I would have preferred to stay with Jasmine, but I'm in no place to voice this.

"Sorry I ruined your vacation." My nose tingles with the onset of tears that I try to hold back but can't. "I ruin everything lately."

The sobs come quick and hard. All the emotion I've stored away when around my parents, trying to spare them more grief, comes flooding out of me. The stupid old-fashioned phone is clunky in my hand and digs into the side of my head as I cry all over it.

"Oh, sweetheart, you don't ruin everything," Gary says when my sobs subside. "It's okay about the vacation. The beach is nice, but your mom and I kind of just want to be home right now. And we want you to be okay."

I grab a tissue from the box on the bedside cabinet that hosts the base of the phone. When I wipe the snot from my nose, the rough tissue scratches across my sensitive skin. "I think I'm okay now." Yesterday this would have been a lie, but today, it's an honest answer.

"I hope so." He goes quiet, and I sense his hesitation from all these miles away and dread what he's about to say. "Your mom and I have had a lot of time to talk these last few days. I guess we both find a beach vacation a little boring." He chuckles, but my stomach is a ball of nerves waiting for the anchor of whatever they've been talking about to drop. He clears his throat. "We're glad to hear you think you're doing okay, but we'd also like you to give therapy another try."

"Oh" is all I manage.

"We know it wasn't your favorite thing," Gary rushes

on, "but we think it could be good for you. We can try different therapists until you find one you like. We can talk about it more once your mom and I are home."

"Okay."

Neither of them ever said anything about therapy after those two initial visits. I thought they didn't care, or notice, that I stopped going. If they had asked me, they might have learned it wasn't because I didn't like it but because I was worried about how much it cost.

I could blame them for my recent spiral, but it's not their fault really. We've all been in a bad place and haven't been able to take care of ourselves, never mind each other. I know they're my parents and all, but I'm old enough to recognize that I'm responsible for my own behavior.

It's the loss of Gemma that's to blame, I think, more than anything else. And no one can make that better.

My mom sounds calmer when Gary puts her on the phone to say goodbye. I reassure her I'm okay and I'll be fine until they get home. Emberly comes in as I hang up the phone with a loud clunk.

Her expression is so dejected, it's almost comical. "Well, I'm grounded for life. It's been nice knowing ya."

I wrap her in a hug, figuring I better get all the Emberly I can before we are separated from each other. I pull out of the embrace, kiss her lips gently, and then rest my forehead against hers.

"We'll get to see each other at school." Admittedly that doesn't feel like enough. "I can watch swim practice, too, and you can bring me home after. You still get to swim, right?"

"Yeah, I still get to swim." We sit together on the bed, holding hands, legs and sides pressed as close to each other as we can get. "I won't be able to give you a ride home, though, or to school in the mornings."

"Oh." I had been counting on having the time alone in the car with her at the very least. I guess it's back to the bus like last year, but it won't be like last year without Gemma squished into the seat next to me.

Emberly rests her head on my shoulder, and I'm determined not to sink into the grief storm.

"My car got flooded," she explains. "It's probably totaled, and my parents are refusing to get me a new one."

"Oh," I say unhelpfully. I'm not used to being the comforting one. "It'll be alright. They can't stay mad forever. We'll sneak off at lunch to have some alone time. It'll be hot."

Emberly's body shakes with laughter, and that's when I breathe a sigh of relief because I believe that we'll get through this. We've been through something raw and much worse than this. Our love will outlast any punishment our parents can give us.

She looks at me with doleful eyes. "My dad said we're taking you to Camille's."

"So I've been told. It'll be fine." I don't want to talk about it with Emberly and bring up all the ugly feelings from last night. "I guess that means Camille got home okay. What about everyone else?"

Emberly squeezes my hand. "The firefighters rescued everyone and got them home. I guess it took a couple of hours."

"We'll all in a shit-ton of trouble."

"We are."

I stare into her eyes, the deep brown holding a world of emotions, only some of which I can read. We lean into each other and are about to kiss when her parents enter, startling us. I move to stand, but Emberly keeps a firm grip on my hand, keeping me in place next to her. It's as if she's telling her parents that even though we fucked up, we're in this together and nothing they do will change that.

When we head out of the hospital, it's hand-in-hand, a force of two against the world. As the sun and humid air hits my face, I feel better than I have in a long time.

Chapter 44

Hurricane Ophelia is no more, having been downgraded to a tropical storm and headed for Canada according to the weather report on the car radio. Though the storm has moved on, it's not without leaving scars behind.

In the bright morning sun, the destruction comes to light. Trees, branches, and debris litter the streets as we make our way to my house to pick up my things for my stay at Camille's. We're diverted down detours several times, yellow sawhorses and flashing police cars blocking roads where power lines are down. Power crews are already working, their orange trucks blocking more roads.

The closer we get to the shoreline, the worse the damage. Some roads are impassable under flood waters and others are coated in a thick layer of sand, evidence of how far the water traveled in the height of the hurricane. My road is far enough away from the Sound that it was spared the flood waters, but my neighborhood wasn't spared the power outages.

When we pull into my driveway, Emberly moves as if to go with me, but her dad says in a stern voice, "You're staying here."

She shrugs apologetically and gives my hand a squeeze.

It's eerily quiet when I open the car door and step out. A random blue tarp is tangled up in one of the ratty old bushes by the front door. It's not ours, so I decide to leave it there in case the owner comes looking for it. Otherwise, the house looks okay, no broken windows or major damage from the hurricane. We got lucky…we were due for some luck.

My next-door neighbors weren't so lucky. An uprooted tree crashed right into the front of their house. They don't appear to be home, and I wonder if they were home when it happened or if they evacuated and will return home to this mess. Either way, it's an unenviable position.

I step around the branches and roofing shingles on the walkway to the front door, my house key and dead phone in hand. Dead because the battery ran out or because of water damage, I'm not sure. Other than my rain jacket, they're the only things that came with me to the party and both have made it home. I've made it home.

Once in my room, I flick the light switch out of habit, but of course, no lights come on. I grab one of Gemma's old swim bags and throw in a few pairs of clothes. My phone charger is plugged in on my nightstand, the empty end dangling off the edge. I add the charger, my tablet, and a couple of books to the bag and take a look around to see if I want anything else.

The jar of sea glass on Gemma's nightstand catches the light and momentarily blinds me. I pick it up and hold it close to my face, staring into the many facets of color, the one piece of red sea glass standing among the greens, whites, and browns. Heavy and clunky as it is, I shove it in between the clothes in the bag. I don't know how long I'll be at Camille's or how hard it'll be to talk with her, but it'll be nice to have a reminder of Gemma with me.

Before I leave the room, I haul my schoolbag onto my shoulders. Then I run my hand along the yellow and white afghan on Gemma's bed. The scent that wafts up is all mine, no trace of Gemma's honeysuckle and chlorine. A lump forms in my throat, but I don't cry.

The last thing I pack is my toiletries. I don't bother

attempting to brush my hair, which has turned kind of crunchy from the dried rain and salt water, though I do brush my teeth. I wish I had thought to take a shower at the hospital where I could've taken advantage of the hot water.

Except for the stairs creaking underneath my tread, the house is silent as a tomb. But no ghost haunting this tomb.

If I'd been asked two weeks ago if I believed in ghosts, I would've laughed and said, "Are you joking?"

Today I have a different answer, one not so clear-cut. Whether Gemma's ghost was real or not, the memories she won't be here to make will haunt me for the rest of my life.

The heats she won't swim at this season's meets. The unbought presents at Christmastime. The prom dress she'll never buy. Graduations, hers at the end of the school year and mine the following year. Weddings. Breakups. Jobs. Maybe babies one day. A million triumphs and failures, big and small.

A lifetime of things that will never happen.

As I close and lock the front door, the bag bumps against it and the jar of sea glass rattles. The sound is a foghorn sounding across the misty sea, a reminder that I'm not alone and people are looking out for me, even when it's hard to sense them. Gemma will always be my big sister, my twin-not-twin, and she'll always be looking out for me.

Beware the storm.

It was a warning that I think had little to do with Hurricane Ophelia. She was warning me to beware of myself. Well, I think I've finally survived my storm of grief.

Back in Emberly's family car, it's an awkward ride to their neighborhood, the only sound the drone of the news radio. Emberly and I hold hands the whole way, my bags tucked on the floor by my feet instead of between us in the back seat.

Camille's house is in the same expensive beach neighborhood as Emberly's. These houses all have a nice view of the water but are up high enough that they don't seem to have sustained any flood damage.

I glimpse the pathway to the long stairway that snakes down to the beach where Emberly and I spent the summer hanging out. I squeeze her hand and send her a secret little smile.

At the end of the block is Camille's house, probably the biggest in the neighborhood. There's a metal gate where you usually have to use a buzzer to get someone to let you in. Today, with workers coming and going as they clean up the property, the gate is left open for anyone to waltz in.

Emberly's dad stops the car at the turnaround of Camille's driveway, which curls around a fancy fountain that looks far less impressive when there's no water flowing through it.

When she hugs me, I whisper, "Call or text me when you can." She kisses my cheek in response.

I thank her dad for the ride and step out of the car. Unlike at my house, it's not quiet here. Chainsaws buzz, and generators hum. Rich people sure do move fast to clean up messes.

My mouth is dry and sweat pools at my armpits when I ring the doorbell. Rosita, the longtime housekeeper for Camille's family, answers.

"Delta! It's good to see you." She pats both my cheeks and gives me that pitying look I've gotten so many times over the last two months. It doesn't bother me as it would have a few days ago; it shows she cares.

I know the way to Camille's room, but Rosita escorts

me there anyway. As she disappears down the hall, I knock on Camille's door. Loud music pounds from inside the room, so I have to knock a second time to be heard.

Camille yells, "Come in!"

I open the door and stand on the threshold. She's lounging on her giant king-sized bed. I stay where I am until she looks up and sees me.

"Oh." She turns down the music. "It's you."

"Yeah." I remain half in and half out of the room.

"My parents told me you're staying here for a few days."

"Yeah." Now that I'm here, I don't know how to start this conversation, so I take my phone from my pocket. "Do you mind if I charge up?"

Camille waves dismissively to her desk. "Sure."

I make myself busy with finding an open plug and rest my phone on the desk. I sit and look at the framed pictures decorating the wall. Gemma is in almost all of them. There's one of the inseparable foursome, a selfie taken by Camille where our faces are big in the frame, smiles spread wide. Seeing it makes my chest tighten and my eyes prickle, but it doesn't send me into a panic spiral.

I take a deep breath because I can and feel Camille watching me.

"I'm glad you're okay," she says.

I look at her and there's honesty behind the serious look on her face. "Thanks..." Camille opens her mouth to say something else, but I stop her. "Wait. Can I speak for a minute?"

She nods, and I dive right into the deep end of the pool rather than inching my way in. "I'm sorry for accusing you of poisoning Gemma. It was stupid and wrong and awful. I've been all kinds of messed up in the head lately, and," I don't really want to go into the whole ghost thing again, so I don't, "well, it took me down a bad path. I'm sorry I took it out on you."

I almost end there but can't help myself from adding, "But I'm still pissed at you for hooking up with Logan."

"I hate myself for it sometimes," Camille whispers. She stares out the window overlooking the Sound and hugs a squishy pink pillow. "Logan doesn't. He says Gemma wouldn't want us to hate ourselves for finding love in our grief."

I still hate either of them invoking what Gemma would've wanted—as if they knew her better than I did—but I bite my lip and keep my mouth shut. We've all been doing what we can to survive, and nothing I say is going to change how Camille and Logan feel about each other.

"Do you want something to eat?" When she finally looks at me, her nose wrinkles. "Or a shower?"

I sniff my pits. "Do I smell that bad?"

She catches my smile and laughs. Then she throws the pink pillow at me. I'm laughing too hard to stop it from hitting my face. That's all it takes for me to know she's forgiven me. I've forgiven her, too, though I'm not giving her and Logan my blessing or anything cheesy like that.

"Do you have hot water?" I ask when we've stopped laughing.

"Yes. The modern miracle of a big-ass generator."

A few minutes later, standing under Camille's fancy rainfall showerhead, I think maybe I do believe in miracles. Gemma certainly didn't get one. But I did...when I became Gemma's sister.

So even though I woke up this morning in the hospital where Gemma died, the weight of her death doesn't feel too heavy to carry for the first time since she died. It's not an overwhelming storm inside me.

And I don't feel guilty about that. I've realized I can't let her death drown me from the inside. My path forward is to honor Gemma in my own way—by showing up every day and making the most of every breath I have left.

Acknowledgments

So many of my books end up being inspired by my sister, Kylene, and *Only Dark Edges* is no exception. Though I've explored grief in some of my other books, this one—though certainly fictional in nearly all aspects—touches the closest upon some of my own feelings of deep grief upon losing Kylene. May the lasting ripples of her life continue to spread.

Having the framework of William Shakespeare's *Hamlet* as inspiration allowed me to stay tethered to the story and kept me from getting lost in the heavy feelings a book like this can bring up. Watching performances of *Hamlet*, particularly the "What a piece of work is a man" speech, by Andrew Scott, Benedict Cumberbatch, Maxine Peake, Kenneth Branagh, and David Tennant brought the Bard's words to life. I highly recommend seeing at least one Shakespeare play live if you get the opportunity, even if you don't consider yourself a fan.

A special thanks to Katlyn Duncan for so many early morning writing/productivity sessions and for providing a safe space to not only hash out story issues but also a place to commiserate on all things writing, publishing, parenting, and life. Most of the first draft of this book was written during National Novel Writing Month, a large chunk of which was written at the Highlights Foundation, two organizations that bring community and support to so many authors. A small but not exhaustive list of writers who have supported me throughout my career include Kai Strand, Patrick Scalisi, Mary Waibel, Julie Zantopoulos, and Amber LaShell. Though they write very different stories than this one, Andi Diehn, Julie Danneberg, Laurel Neme, and Laura Perdew always offer solid critiques, advice, and camaraderie.

Final thanks are always reserved for my family—my sisters and brother, mom and dad, nieces and nephews, in-laws, and extended family who cheer me on and inspire me. And, of course, my own personal group of superheroes in Batman, The Boy, The Prince, and The Gentleman.

About the Author

Award-winning author Katie L. Carroll always says she began writing at a very sad time in her life after her sister Kylene unexpectedly passed away. The truth is Katie has been writing her whole life, and it was only after Kylene's death that she realized she wanted to pursue writing for kids and teens as a career. Since then writing has taken her to many wonderful places —both real and imagined. She's had many jobs in her lifetime, including newspaper deliverer, hardware store cashier, physical therapy assistant, and puzzle magazine editor. She works in Connecticut from her home that is filled with the love and laughter of her sons and husband.

If you enjoyed *Only Dark Edges*, be sure to write a review on your favorite book retail sites. Katie is also the author of the award-winning YA fantasy *Elixir Bound* and its sequel *Elixir Saved*. Her other books are the middle grade novels *Witch Test* and *Pirate Island;* picture books *Mommy's Knight Before Christmas*, illustrated by Phoebe Cho, and *The Bedtime Knight*, illustrated by Erika Baird; and the nonfiction children's book *Selfies From Mars: The True Story of Mars Rover Opportunity*. For more about Katie and her books, visit her website at katielcarroll.com.

Find Katie L. Carroll online

Website: https://katielcarroll.com/
TikTok: @katielcarrollauthor
Twitter: @katielcarroll
Instagram: @katielcarrollauthor
Facebook: www.facebook.com/katielcarrollauthor/

www.ingramcontent.com/pod-product-compliance
Lightning Source LLC
Chambersburg PA
CBHW031236210726
48287CB00003B/796